POWDER
& PAINT

Anthony Moss

Honeybee
Books

Published by Honeybee Books
Broadoak, Dorset
www.honeybeebooks.co.uk

Printed in the UK using paper from sustainable sources

ISBN: 978-1-910616-47-5

Thanks to my wife Miranda
for her help, support and ideas whilst I wrote this book.

CHAPTER ONE

I was sitting, just looking. Looking and listening to their jokey conversations, taking the mickey in the main. Not much has changed.

"Give me another bourbon, Sam!" I asked.

"Haven't you had enough for tonight, old man?" came his usual reply.

Sam was about the same age as me. He had worked behind the bar here at what would seem like forever. Like me he had seen most things, most kinds come through this bar. His sun-cracked face and greasy hair make him look like he had spent his life out on a ship sailing the high seas. Instead, like me, he has only really been here. It's somewhat of a cliché, but if the walls in this place could talk... Every night I just think, as I am now, of all the stories that have walked into this place. When I say stories, I mean just that. Not just people who happen to come in here for the occasional drink, but people who in their own right are a story. Some of these stories would not be good for the ear, so it's probably better you don't ask how their story started – let alone finished.

Fair to say most are not the usual 'Hollywood' happy ever after.

I glance around and remember how the now faded curtains, and pictures that hang somewhat askew, were once bright and vibrant in colour. Now, they kind of add to the atmosphere of this bygone bar on the harbour front of this far away little port that really no one has heard of. The smoke hangs heavy, a mixture of strong American Marlboro intertwined with the even stronger aroma of cigar. No wonder the décor has faded over the years, it hasn't had a breath of fresh air waft over it in decades.

Sam pours me the drink, as he did earlier, leaving yet another bottle on the bar. The same as he has done for the last God knows how long. I take a sip; look around at the 'beautiful people'. There have always been beautiful people; at least there have been here. Some things have changed with the passing of time, but not all. Yes, sure, they now have fancy modern cars parked up outside. They have their designer clothes, sporting the brand name all over the front and back, sometimes both. I smile to myself; there were always designer clothes except the beautiful people of my time wore the labels on the inside. They talk of the day's events, the challenges they had faced against all odds.

"The wind took the sail right out of my hands!"

"Oh it got so hot I had to spend the whole afternoon in the villa."

Somehow the challenges of today would have been a pleasure of yesterday. Eleven thirty, now it's getting busy. Just like the old days, always filling up around this time. Difference now is they come from their five star hotels, having eaten a dinner that would feed the average family for a week, and then it's out to sample some of the local culture.

There was never any local culture here. We were all nomads passing through, looking for an escape. An escape in some cases for genuine reasons, reasons that were rarely spoken about.

I slide back towards my favourite corner table, over to the right of the bar, just up a few steps overlooking the small dance floor. It has a good vantage point of the whole bar area and doorway. This had proved to be a benefit over the years, well not so much recently, but certainly when I first came here. I could always duck out back if someone I had, shall we say 'not got on too well with' the night before had come in after me – literally, after me. This had always been my eleven thirty spot; I could people-watch in peace.

Where is he from? What does she do? The questions have always been in my head. Sitting here as I do every night, I end up in my usual un-offensive drunken slumber. I guess it's a combination of the booze, the smoke and the heat. It was always so darned hot in here.

Watching again I notice a man heading my way, he looks almost lost. Not lost in the sense of not knowing where he is, but lost in the sense of not fitting in.

"Mind if I join you?" he asks. An American, I thought. That's all I need, some young sycophantic American punk who wants to befriend and probably humour an old guy such as me.

I nod, gesturing toward a chair for him.

Sitting down he smiles cautiously. Like me, he's tanned from the sun; his combat trousers and shirt look almost reminiscent of a bygone era. His clothes, unlike the combat trousers of some of the other clientele, are not fashion designed. His are worn for a more practical use. I glanced down to look at his footwear. Black boots shin high, laced firmly to the top. He nodded his head to one side seeing that I had cast an eye up and down. His face had a question-ing expression, almost a frown as if to say 'Well?' I didn't comment but just took a sip of my bourbon. Looking up from my glass I focused on his short crew cut blond hair. His well chiselled jawline was easily visible even in this near dark lighting.

"Just passing through, or looking for eternal peace?" I ask him.

Smiling, he pauses before replying, "Oh, it ain't the peace bit, that's for sure."

"How about you, old man, are you looking for eternal peace or what?"

"I wish I knew. I came here 1946 looking for the peace bit I guess, but I ain't found it yet. Least every time I thought I had found it someone or something took it away from me."

"Tell me more," he asked.

I looked into to his eyes. For someone of his age I couldn't help but think he had seen a lot. He might not tell me now, but I figured given time he just might.

"How about you, look around in here, what do you see?" I replied. I moved my head quite deliberately as to demonstrate what I wanted him to do. "What do you see?" I asked again. Before he could answer I cut in. I was known for that, it's one of my weaknesses. "You see people, just people not knowing where they have come from, and certainly not knowing where they are going."

I then started my story. I told him how I had come to South America, arriving in August of 1946. It was hot that year. Not that I wasn't acclimatised. The war had seen me in southern Italy, and then on to North Africa with Monty.

After the war-torn years, I went back home to England to find, not the place I had left, but a place of complete devastation. It was not just the flattened buildings, but also the whole devastation of life. The woman I had left as my wife before I went off to war, was more a stranger than someone I had betrothed my life to. And my son, a bonny boy, had come to know another as his dad. It held nothing for me, nothing that I could remember. For once I was alone, free of people in my life. I took stock of things and thought if I take off who will notice I'm missing? No one came to mind.

With my savings in one hand, 'war wages' as I affectionately called them, I hitched a lift down to Southampton, taking the first freighter to anywhere. This place ended up being anywhere! Working as a deckhand I kept myself in cigarettes and booze. Looking back it was hard work, but the prospect of paradise made it more bearable.

Six weeks later, after leaving Southampton, I arrived to a melee of noise and confusion. Walking down the gangplank, which I can still picture, I was thinking 'what the hell have I done?' People were shouting but the words were all a mess to me. As I walked down the gangplank along with the rest of my fellow crew members, hawkers came from what seemed like all directions, offering their wares to us. I guess that our pale European complexions were like a big neon sign to them, flashing brightly with either pounds sterling or maybe American dollars. Either way as we walked down the gangplank we were surrounded by men and women wanting to sell me anything from small ceramic pots to brightly coloured shirts and wood-carved figures. I squinted from the bright midday sun. I pulled the fedora down to shade my eyes. The same hat goes where I go, even today. I have few possessions of value, never have, but my fedora is definitely one I do have! I had landed in Cartagena on the northern coast of Colombia and not really knowing where on the map I was other than somewhere damn hot and sticky. After a couple of weeks dossing in a quayside boarding house I made my way across the country to the Pacific coast – which I was told was by far the prettiest coast you will ever see. Mind you, the man who told me that only had one eye, and from what I remember he was nearly always blind drunk when I saw him in the few weeks I was up there.

Anyway, I hitched a lift or two and finally arrived here in one hell of a monsoon. Dripping wet through with all my worldly goods in a small kit bag I stumbled into this place. Los Santos has been my home ever since. Guess now I will never go back to England, wouldn't recognize it anyway!

My new friend looked tired. He sipped the last drops from his bottle of beer and placed it very slowly and precisely on to the tattered beer mat. Quite when these dog-eared mats first came out on to the tables advertising various brands of beer was beyond me. A good rub-down and re-varnish of the tables would go a long way to improve the décor – as opposed to the miniscule gesture to enhance our surroundings.

"Am I boring you, young man?"

"No, no not at all, but I would like to find my room. I am getting tired but not of your story. Can we continue another time, tomorrow perhaps? Where will I find you?" he asked.

"What makes you so sure I want to meet you?" I replied.

"Oh, I kinda somehow think you do. I gotta feelin' you and me are gonna hit it off just real good. Here, let me buy you a drink, bourbon is it? I'll get the barman to bring it over."

As he rose from his chair I noticed the size of this man. He stood a good six feet tall, he smiled and made his way down the few steps from my viewpoint and squeezed his way back towards the bar. It was only when he leaned over the bar to shout my drink order into Sam's ear that I noticed how loud it was. The music was up to its normal ear-piercing levels and whether it was the bourbon or the dreamlike world of an old man and his memories I don't know, but, for a few brief moments, I had gone back in time to my days when even around here things were a lot less hectic. Or were they?

Sam brought me my drink; I looked again for the nameless young man to thank him, if only with a gesture of the hand in the air. But, like my youth, he had gone. Oh well, I thought, what's new?

I drank up, but unlike other nights, I wouldn't be waking up here in the Los Santos Hotel's bar at dawn. Tonight I would make my way along the old beach road back to my bungalow overlooking the sea. The same bungalow I had built back in '48.

Stumbling into my old faithful jeep I started her up and gingerly headed out of the harbourside and towards the coast road. At this time of night, well 2 am in the morning, the only other road users would be bats. They sweep in between the high banks of the pine road feasting on the midges that swarm under the branches of the majestic trees. I had driven this road at this time of night for close on thirty years, and almost every night this last week. Selecting third and then guiding it into top gear, my trusty old machine edged up over the crest of the pine road ridge where I pulled over to glance back at the sleeping town and harbour. Two hours from now at daybreak it would spark into life when the first of the fishing boats would head off out for the day. Not that I would be party to any of that. My day usually started around midday or maybe eleven-thirty if I really wanted to make an early start. I looked out to sea. It was black.

Pushing the gearstick into first I eased the clutch and headed off again. The headland road really was heaven at this time of night. On the other side of the hill the sky was even blacker now but awash with stars. As I got to the bottom of the hill I glanced across to the beach which at this point reached all the way to my bungalow and fringed the road. The small waves licked up on to the shore. The moon not full but still bright, and assisted by the millions of stars, it guided me back along the dusty road.

I fell on to the bed where all my dreams had come true, at least in my head. It was hot again, the ceiling fan span above my head buzzing as it went. I wondered if I would see my new friend again to continue our, or at least my, conversation as he had said, or was he just humouring an old man? I certainly hoped not.

CHAPTER TWO

The next morning came all too quickly. The sunrays looked like pillars between the shutters that covered the outside of my windows. The dusty sand of the beach never seemed to settle. Squinting through one eye I could see it clearly in each ray of sun.

Getting to my feet I undressed from my evening attire and made my way to the shower. Would the water be hot this morning? A thought I had every morning for the last thirty or so years. Warm as usual. It was ten thirty in the morning, early for me. I got the coffee on and sat out on the veranda overlooking the beach.

My view to the left was the open stretch of the bay sweeping the two and a half miles or so back to my favourite watering hole. In fact my only watering hole, the Los Santos Hotel. Not so much a hotel these days but more of a refuge for, shall we say, the lower budget traveller. The young lads are beginning to turn up now as always. Surf is getting up. Now, though, they arrive in their Japanese pickup trucks. It used to be on bicycles and their boards were hollowed-out tree trunks. It is still a beautiful sight for all of that – the white sand, blue sea beyond, green grass and palms which offer welcome shade as the sun rises ever more.

To my right I could see what I called Colditz. This was to me the modern day epitome of the modern day paradise. 'A taste of the real culture' I read once in a brochure shown to me by a passing American tourist. Wall to wall food and drink, weekly cultural entertainment brought to them wrapped like a gift to prise open, to play with like a child and then just as easily toss aside.

The air-conditioned rooms at the five-star Kumota Plaza Hotel offered all the creature comforts of the great cities of today's world. Fitness gyms and beauty parlours cater for their every whim. They go home to their loved ones spouting of the fortunes of the travel experiences they have encountered on this vacation. I can hear them saying, 'She has got one of the best sun tans money can buy for free, and the masseur commented on how he had only ever seen a body as firm as hers when working on a much younger woman.' He meanwhile, has improved his handicap down to a credible five.

Still, I guess they are happy in their own little way. They certainly make people here happy, splashing their dollars around.

My humble abode has always been a bit of a sore point with the management of the Kumota Plaza Hotel. The little ramshackle bungalow does not figure in their scheme of local culture. An old house was seen by the hotel's owners as a relic of days gone by, from an era that is best forgotten. I was a sort of ailing real-life adventurer and explorer.

Keep going on the beach road beyond the Plaza and you come into the lush green agricultural area of these parts. The landscape changes dramatically from the sweeping open beach with a backdrop of pine forests to wide open flat plains that are farmed for rice, cotton and root vegetables such as sweet potato and corn. Rumour has it there are other crops out there but these are not for the regular family table and chances are they will never be consumed here but far away from these parts. But that just now is another story all together.

"Hope that coffee is hot and strong?"

Startled, I turned around. I see a welcome face from last night.

"I tried the front door but got no reply, so I thought I'd try round the back here."

"Oh, right, umm, good to see you again, young man," I said nervously. I was surprised to say the least at seeing him standing there leaning on the side of my veranda. There was a silent pause. I felt myself tilt my head to one side, as I looked him straight in the eye. Many thoughts raced through my mind. Who was he really? What did he want, if anything? If it's money, he's come knocking on the wrong door. My wealth went long ago on the flip of a card in a game of poker one night during the monsoon season of 1957.

"Joe Brampton," I said eventually, introducing myself.

"Hi Joe, I'm Scott Kowlowski," he replied, offering his hand to shake mine. I couldn't help but notice his firm grip almost crush my knuckles. He had a workman's hands. There were a couple of scrapes to the back of his hand and I noticed his broken or even bitten nails. He didn't work in an office, that's for sure. I thought I had a good handshake, but this guy really could shake a man's hand.

"Hi Scott, let's get that coffee."

We went inside through the patio doors, into the sitting room and then into my small kitchen. All the time I could sense his mighty presence, but at no time did I feel threatened. This man had compassion. Almost nervously I got a mug out of the cupboard. Thank God, I thought, there is a clean one. It was a rare event in my house to find anything much washed and dried, let alone put away. Having poured the coffee we move back on to the veranda.

"Pull up a chair, Scott." I watched him again as I had last night, but this time being able to focus somewhat better. He picked up the chair as I would have at his age, effortlessly. Now it's all I can do to slide it along to where I want it. "I didn't think I'd see you again, young man, not voluntarily anyhow."

He smiled again. I noticed he had quite a dimple on the

right of his mouth, low down on his cheek.

"Well, believe it or not what you had to say I found really interesting. You have a story to tell, not a story to dream."

"How did you find me?" I asked.

"Oh, I just asked the first person I bumped into this morning down at the quayside. Seems everyone knows you or certainly knows of you. I think the chap is called Stephan, he works..."

I interrupted him. "He works on the quayside. He also knows better than to tell strangers where I live. Wait till I see him!" I said with conviction.

Thirty years ago that would have been true, but now? Come on, I thought to myself, those days of ducking and diving are long gone. Who was I kidding? I quickly corrected myself as the atmosphere had become quite prickly.

"I was just joking, Scott. That old Polish bugger, I'll give him what for when I next see him," I quipped. The tension relaxed and I continued to question my guest. "But how did you get out here? I didn't hear a car or bus."

"Oh I walked. It's a fantastic bit of coast, but I reckon you know that."

"Well yes I do, but you say you walked it? What time did you leave?"

"Only about an hour ago, it's not that far really, is it?"

"Might not be for you, but for me it's the equivalent of a route march, especially in the heat. With a name like Kowlowski I think it's safe to say you're not from around these parts, are you, Scott?" That smile, almost smirk-like, provoked something in the back of my mind.

"No, California, USA is home for me. I'm just here on a sort of vacation."

Why do Americans always assume that we, as non-Americans, don't know which country their home state is in? I guess that is just one of life's little mysteries.

"You say you are here on a sort of vacation? You intrigue me, tell me more. I think it's your turn to do some talking; I did all the running last night if I remember. I certainly haven't had my daily bourbon quota just yet. It's early even for me."

"I'm here to find someone. Perhaps I should say evidence of someone. I don't think they are still alive. But if they were, maybe someone like you would know them, or at least know of them. I hope you don't mind, but well that's why I sat with you last night. I've been here for a few days. You were the first person I have seen that might help me. As I said, I hope you don't mind?"

There was a time when I might not have been so forth-coming or open to people until I really got to know them. But now, my first thought was, what the hell, I'm too ancient to mind. I have no real friends to confide in these days, they have all gone, back to England or the States long ago, and then those that stayed just slipped away.

A long silence prevailed. I looked at him with a blank expression. He looked ever more hesitant.

"Tell me, who is it you are you looking for, Scott?"

His smile erupted once more. "Oh wow! You'll help me find who I'm looking for? Oh wow, Joe, thank you. His name... his name is Robert Koke. He is or was my uncle – my father's younger brother, not that my father is alive, though. That's why I'm here. Apart from my younger sister, Uncle Bob and his wife Louise are the only family I have. My sister Emma has been married now for almost eight years I guess. She has two kids, a boy and a younger girl. I talk to them now and again on the phone and visit like once in a blue moon. As I said, I live in California; she's in upstate New York which as you probably know is the other side of the country to me. It's a bit more than a quick bus ride and what with my work and my bachelor lifestyle we are worlds apart.

"My dad always said we were different. Emma only wanted

the house, the kids, and the husband. Me, I always wanted more, more from life than just that anyway. So here I am a kind of modern day adventurer or even a bounty hunter looking for my treasure. Not a financial treasure I hasten to add."

"You've come to the wrong house if it is finance you want!" I cut in.

"No, no my bounty will come in the shape of knowing what went on before. Dad showed me letters from Uncle Bob. Letters that stirred something inside me from an early age to break out of suburbia, break out into the big unknown world. You see like my sister and me, Dad and Bob were worlds apart in their lives too. They both served in Europe for the Army, but Dad came home to California, met Mom and the rest is history. He got a steady job, nice house in a nice neighbourhood, two kids, living the American dream."

After a pause, Scott continued. "I'd heard the name of this Uncle Bob and Aunt Louise usually around Christmas or around Emma's or my birthday. A card and some weird looking money would arrive. I say weird money because for a kid of nine growing up in the States at that time, there was no other world out there. As far as we were concerned, anything and everything we needed was right there in the US in our back yard as it were within a hundred mile radius. He would also always say pretty much verbatim with each delivered letter that the money Bob and Louise had sent had probably been won in a poker game. Mom, as always, would quietly calm him as only she could.

"It was several years later when I was around fourteen or fifteen that Dad brought out the letters from his bedside cabinet. So for all his cursing he had kept them for years. Mom told me how he had been slightly jealous of his younger brother of two years, for the life he had chosen to take after the war in comparison to his own. He never had had that adventurous streak like Bob, and Aunt Louise would have followed him over burnt coals to be by his side. I believe he changed his surname to Koke simply because the locals couldn't pronounce Kowlowski."

A shiver ran down my neck. I went almost cold. So that's why I kinda recognised that smirk. This was Bob and Louise Koke's nephew. Bob Koke had a dimple the size of a dolphin's blowhole on his right cheek, those same narrow eyes too, when I come to think of it.

"Yes, that's true!" I said. "We have much to talk about, young Scott. But first I think you should know that neither your Uncle Bob nor your gorgeous Aunt Louise is around. Hell if they were… oh, if only they were, yep, if only they were."

I told him of how we had all met one evening at, back then, the only hotel on this stretch of beach called the Kumota. It was a lot different in those heady days of 1948. Full of people from all over like me looking for some kind of escape or freedom. Freedom, after what was like a nightmare that had lasted six years across the world, especially in Europe. There were mainly Americans and English, a few French and even one or two Polish. It was rumoured though, back then and still even today, that not a million miles from here some Germans had settled after the war but for very different reasons to ours. We just wanted to get away from the hell that was war and start a fresh life for ourselves. Their reasons were more sinister. Story has it they were wanted for the war crimes they had committed back in Europe in the concentration camps.

The Polish didn't stay long, many making their way to the USA, the French too disappeared by the 50s going even further north into Canada, no doubt seeking out their distant relations.

It was one of those impromptu nights when people unwittingly drop all their fronts or barriers and let their hair down. The people just became people, enjoying life, the value of life. Like a New Year's party at midnight, except it was August.

Bob and Louise Koke owned the old swinging Los Santos Hotel. They had it about five or six months, sinking all their savings into a run-down ramshackle hotel, which in their mind's eye had 'great potential'.

After my arrival in 1946 I spent the first three weeks drinking in a bar along one of the side streets away from the quayside. The Mermaid's Resting Place, I had a room there as well. But I had heard how there was great jazz being played by some ex-American GIs in a hotel called the Kumota Beach in the centre of town. Just like today, it stands in that pretty tree lined plaza.

Hoping to find some excitement, I took myself over to the Los Santos Hotel having a drink at each bar that I passed, eventually arriving to the sound of some really hopping tunes. Looking in, I could see there were people dancing and drinking, and just having a great time. I made my way to the bar and ordered my usual bourbon. Looking around I fought my way through the crowd to a small table overlooking the dance floor. I spotted an empty table and wandered over and sat down. That table and me were to become all too familiar with each other over the coming years. Smirking to myself I pictured that first evening in the Los Santos Hotel.

My first encounter was slightly fraught to say the least. Half-cut as usual on the very cheap bourbon I had made a pass at the pretty barmaid, who was fighting her way back to the bar with some empty glasses.

"I only like my men tall, and looking at you, well you've got some growing to do!" she quickly retorted.

A polite but firm put down, I thought. But not one to give

up easily I followed her through the crowded bar area to the dance floor. She half-turned around and saw me out of the corner of her deep blue eyes. This time she stood and looked directly at me, smiling a smile that said a thousand words. Like a lamb to the slaughter I smiled back, but before I could say one of my infamous chat-up lines she turned again and called to the man behind the bar.

"There's a chap here who would like to make your acquaintance, darling." I stood there, all five foot seven inches of me, and watched as from behind the bar a man of a mountain came around holding out his hand to shake mine. A hand that was firm and strong,

"Hi, Robert Koke, I run the Kumota Beach pleased to meet you. Oh, you've met Louise, my wife."

"Aaargh yea, yes," I said. "Joe, Joe Brampton."

Shaking his hand I felt a feeling inside of well-being, this was going to be the start of a great and hopefully long friendship. We chatted about this and that, just the usual pleasantries. After my initial introduction I was, too say the least, nervous. But my fear had soon passed after finding out I could, for the first time in a long time, relate to this gentle giant of a man.

As time went by my regular visits to the Kumota Beach saw the relationship grow even more. Bob and I would take off in a small fishing boat that I had won in game of poker with an American – just occasionally my poker games paid off.

I would pick Bob up from the hotel around three in the afternoon, just after the lunchtime rush. He would promise Louise faithfully that he would be back for around six thirty latest and with supper to boot.

"Oh yes, I'll believe it when I see it from you two. The only thing you ever come back with, Bob Koke, is a hangover when you set off with that villain Brampton!"

Sure enough she was right. We would cast our lines over the stern once we were out a mile or so. I remember the views looking back inland along the coast. They were fantastic. Away to our left of the pine road headland the sweeping surf thundered on to the sands there. Out here, straight ahead from the town's harbour, the sea was just a gentle swell, that when you have had a couple or so to wet your thirst, lulls you into a comforting slumber as if you are swinging in a cradle rather than lolloping about in a boat. Here we could put the world, or at least our world, to right, sipping bourbon. I always kept a bottle on board, and just as Louise had predicted we'd get slowly oiled.

We always waited till near dark, as on these occasions the lights leading into the narrow channel of the harbour mouth illuminated our pathway home. The odd times we did make the effort to come home in daylight meant we'd end up landing, or should I say going aground, on a mud bank just off the east side of the harbour entrance. So, armed with this information, in our state of merriment we always came home in the dark.

As time went by I boosted my income, which in the main was gained from playing poker, by doing odd jobs around the hotel for Bob and Louise. Besides paying me, Louise would make me a meal, which I would take with them most evenings before the night-time rush.

The work paid for me to save to get this old bungalow built. Bob once offered for me to move into the attic space of the hotel. It was huge, but I didn't want to impose more than I had. Anyway, for the first time in my life, I was beginning to become responsible. Responsible enough to want to make an effort in my appearance, in my attitude toward the work Bob provided me, which in turn gave me the building blocks for my new life with my new friends.

"Oh, Scott, I have so many stories, so many memories of

that time."

Images flashed through my head, faces from that era. Big Georgie the barman Bob hired. Georgie was born old. I swear from when he walked into the bar for the first time until he left in a box some eighteen years later he didn't age. Like so many, poor old Georgie had gone. He had passed away one Sunday night after one hell of a weekend session.

"We had some great times and laughs along the way. You mentioned your dad keeping the letters from Bob. I can't say if he ever wanted to go back to the States, not even for a visit. We were all like that. All of us down here didn't talk or even wonder 'what if', I guess we had become so wrapped up in our own world here. Louise, I know for a fact, had no family to go back home too. At least not much after 1950 or so, that's when her mother's sister had passed away. If I remember right, her parents died when she was quite young and she took to travelling around the States singing in bars and hotels. There was the occasional time when Bob was able to get her up and sing in the Kumota Beach. She was great." Again the image of the memory became vivid in my mind's eye.

"Want another coffee?" I asked. "I need a good few to get me awake. Mind you, my days are not as hectic as they used to be."

Going in to the kitchen I noticed the time, ten to twelve. "Scott, how do you fancy lunch? I know a great little seafood place, down on the quay."

"Yeh sounds good!"

"Well let's skip that coffee and go now."

"Okay, lead the way, Joe!"

I put the cups in the sink and grabbed my hat and jeep keys off the table.

"Let's go!"

"Don't you kinda have to lock up?"

I smiled and mumbled, "I haven't done it in forty years. There is nothing here worth having, except some old clothes and a pile of memories, and they all go where I go! You drive, I'll direct."

CHAPTER THREE

We turned out of the drive, on to the beach road. By now, like every day at this time, the afternoon breeze was beginning to get up. The palms swayed gently, their shade welcome in the searing heat, especially for those on the beach. Looking away to our left towards the entrance to the Kumota Plaza Hotel, we saw the various hawkers plying their locally made wares to the tourists, who were walking back to the hotel for lunch. We turned to our right, back along the beach road glancing across at the surfers as we went. As we drove between the pine trees we rode in silence. My thoughts drifting back again reminding me of times gone by having just had some of those memories rekindled by Scott's visit this morning. The little motor in my jeep purred along quite happily despite its rusty and dirty appearance. With only the occasional whoosh overpowering its sound as the increasing wind blew through, heavy with needles pine trees. The road wound its way down hill towards the town.

"We need to follow the road through, way along the quayside. You see that big blue and white trawler? Park up over there."

The Ocean's Pantry canopy shaded the diners who were already seated outside.

"Looks pretty busy, will we need to book a table?"

"Oh, don't worry about that, they will always have a table for me."

We crossed the road. One of the waiters approached Scott whose large bulk obscured his view of me.

"Do you want a table for one, sir?" asked the waiter, but as I caught Scott up and stood by his side he added, "Oh Mr Joe, how are you? We have not seen you in a while now. A table for two is it? And will you want a nice shaded table, back there in the corner? How will that be for you, Mr Joe? Okay I hope?"

"Just the job, Enrico, thanks. And yeah, it has been a while, but who knows, maybe that will change from now on."

I turned to Scott. "See, you don't need to book." I smiled at him; he smiled back with that gentle boyish smirk of his, shaking his head as we followed Enrico to the table in the corner.

The gentle breeze licked around the building here, making it more pleasant to dine at this time of the day. Not as strong as it was up on the coast road, just pleasant, just right.

"I will get madam for you. She will want to see you for sure!"

"Who is madam?" Scott asked.

"Madam is someone you should get to know." He looked at me with a puzzled expression only for it to be broken as we heard voices from inside the restaurant.

"Oops, sounds to me like someone's gotten the wrong order," Scott muttered

"No, that's no wrong order," I corrected. It was the voice and language of an excited Spanish-speaking woman called Romana.

"Uncle Joe! Where 'ave you been? I 'ave not seen you in a week or even more. You must come to town at least once a week; if only so I know you have had one good meal between your drinking sprees."

Romana stood there beaming with elegance, her long black hair tied back off of her face. Romana was tall, five foot ten I guess. She was born in the spring of 1949.

I just stood there for a moment, just looking at what

happiness was. Scott also stood, just looking, ready to offer a greeting. A few seconds lapsed.

"Well, Uncle Joe, are you going to introduce me?"

Before I could say anything Scott had stepped forward a pace holding out his hand to introduce himself. In doing so he knocked the chair to his right on the next table.

"I hope you have not been teaching him any of your bad drinking habits, Uncle," Romana joked. She had seen me many a time after having one too many at the old hotel bar.

"Scott, Scott Kowlowski," said Scott. Romana gingerly put her hand out to meet and shake his, at the same time a look of hesitation appeared on her face.

"Kowlowski?" she said turning to look at me but with a questionable tone in her voice.

"Is there a problem?" asked Scott.

"No Scott, no problem. You see I didn't know how to tell you before, but…"

I hesitated this time. Romana now looked just as concerned as Scott. Looking at them both, I felt awkward to say the least.

"But you see, Scott, Romana is your cousin – Bob and Louise's only child. There, I've said it now!"

"Wow, well how do you do, I guess." Scott sat back down. "I never knew, Dad had spoken about Uncle Bob and Aunt Louise, but never that they had a daughter… and that I had a cousin!"

"It's a bit early in the day really, I think," Romana said breaking the silence. "But you look like you could do with a drink. Bourbon, Scott?"

He just looked up at Romana almost with a dazed expression and nodded a 'Yes'.

"No need to ask Uncle Joe," she said turning back towards the restaurant going into the bar. Scott just sat there shaking his head repeatedly.

"I never knew. It just didn't cross my mind that they had children."

Romana returned with a bottle and three glasses.

"You don't normally drink bourbon," I said to her.

"Oh, I think I will today, Uncle." She poured us all a drink.

"Well, here's to what? I say we drink to the past, present and future!" I toasted, raising my glass.

In one swift action she had downed the shot and was pouring herself another.

"You see, Uncle Joe, I did listen to you sometimes. 'Never taste it, just swallow it, unlike life.'" She smiled, her expression was more relaxed again, and she had that twinkle in her eye.

I explained to Romana my chance meeting the night before with Scott and our subsequent meet this morning.

"I didn't know how to approach the subject, either with you, Scott, or you, Romana."

"Planning never was your strong point was it, Uncle?"

Scott all this time was transfixed by Romana. He had also helped himself to several shots of the bourbon.

"Wow. Where do we go from here?" he asked in a somewhat confused tone.

"Scott, my dear boy, I'll tell you where we go from here. We grab the menu and order some lunch. Here at the Ocean's Pantry you will have some of the best seafood to be had anywhere on this godforsaken planet of ours. We will eat!"

"Mama was right. Uncle Joe never has problems to deal with, he side steps them and then moves forward. Don't forget that, Scott. Enrico!" she yelled. "Two seafood platter specials and some red wine please. And Enrico, before you say it should be white, this is for my uncle Joe!" She turned to me and smiled.

"Anything lighter in colour than rosé is water, is that right, Uncle?" I smiled and nodded back to her.

"Please excuse me; I must sort out a few things in the kitchen – your fresh crayfish for a start."

Romana got up and as she did, so did Scott.

"I'm sorry I seem a bit vague, but I think like you, I'm in shock," said Scott.

"Oh I'm not too shocked. You see, Scott, when someone appears out of the blue with my uncle Joe, well let's just say that after all these years I've learned to expect anything. But, to be honest unlike you, I did know I had cousins in America! We'll talk later I promise, but right now I must sort out the kitchen."

Enrico appeared again, this time holding a tray with two beers, a bottle of red wine and a jug of water, balanced precariously on one hand, his fingers poised like upturned table legs. He weaved between the tables, the glasses clinking on the bottles as he came towards us.

"Oh great news!" he exclaimed. "Madam has just told me!"

Scott still looked slightly dazed whilst being reminded of the earlier revelations.

"She also says no more bourbon! If you must drink it has to be beer. The water," he said turning to Scott, "is for you. She also says you would probably only want this anyway!"

I grinned knowing Romana had no intentions of having two drunks on her hands at her restaurant at lunchtime.

"Come on, Scott, have a drink. Don't be shocked, think positive," I said.

"Yeah, you're right." He poured himself a beer raising his glass toward me.

"This calls for a toast! To whatever the hell else life has to surprise us with!"

"To life," I answered

Romana appeared again carrying a large tray.

"I've done you a selection of, well everything really. Everything that is from our local waters that is!"

There were mussels, oysters, squid, lobster and other

delights from the sea around these parts. Enrico brought out a platter of rice surrounded by a fresh salad.

"Wow, it seems a shame to eat this, what a display of colour," chirped Scott.

I must say it never ceased to amaze me the beautiful presentation of a meal Romana and her staff would lovingly put before their clientele. Lunch soon rolled by dominated with endless conversation about our lives. I sat back now and then and just looked at Scott and Romana. They laughed and joked with each other. Romana had a sparkle in her eye. I could not help but think, would this chance meeting lead to a new relationship that would or could be full of complications for both of them? I sincerely hoped not.

Just adding the odd acknowledgement to their chatter, I looked out to the harbour where by now the sun was slipping once again into the distant west. I dreamed again as I often do and also hoped that they had learned. Learned that life is too complicated sometimes and you must go with your heart and not your head. As Romana had said at lunchtime, maybe I do just side-step problems, but then again, I follow my heart.

"Joe, Joe!"

"Sorry, Scott, I was away with my thoughts."

"So I see. Look I must get back to the hotel and freshen up. Can I give you a lift back home? I can then pick you up again at around say nine thirty. Romana has promised to take us all to a little bar at the other side of the harbour. She says you know it, the Catfish and Shark, it sounds great!"

"Look, you two don't want me tagging along. You have some fun on your own. I can always see you again tomorrow."

"You weren't listening to a thing we said were you, Uncle?" Romana cut in. "I said you would say that. I saw you, looking out to the west. Are you dreaming again of days gone by? About you and Daddy getting up to no good in that old boat of yours I bet?"

"Yeah you could say something like that." I smiled.

"Well, if you had been listening, you would have heard how I said that you could team up with Harry, um, whatever his name is. You know who I mean; he still plays the clarinet over there. Goodness knows you used to make enough noise with him and that silly looking drummer from New York."

"It's Harry Irving, and the even sillier looking Josh Barker. They're not still around are they?"

"Alive and kicking the both of them at the Catfish. C'mon, Uncle, let Scott take you home, freshen up and have a couple hours rest. We haven't many bookings tonight, and anyway I have already arranged for Enrico's wife, Maria, to help out and keep my business in one piece for the night."

"If I didn't know better I'd say you were as cunning as your old dad. Although sometimes, Romana, I think he might have taken lessons off of you. Okay, you win, I would love to come. Anyway I haven't seen those two old renegades in ages; it will be good to catch up. I might even bring along my horn and give it a blow with them!"

Scott took me back home, and a couple hours later he had returned, clean-shaven and spruced up.

"Meeting someone special?" I mused and watched his face show off that big dimple again. Like an excited kid, Scott talked non-stop all the way to the Ocean's Pantry where he had arranged to pick up Romana. Quite what he was saying I don't really recall. I was too happy with myself to listen. For the first time, in a long time, life was being kind to me. I just sat back and took in the scenery.

Romana lived upstairs above the restaurant in her apartment. Although many people, whilst having a meal, had enjoyed the views across the harbour they would often then ask if there were any rooms.

"Yes and…no!" was more often or not the answer. "Yes, there are rooms upstairs, but they are not always for rent."

She had never actively advertised that there were rooms available. It really depended on who was asking and how they had more or less behaved whilst dining. Romana's opinion would determine whether she would allow them to be an overnight guest in what was, after all, her house.

Enrico greeted us at the front of the restaurant. We were able to park right outside.

"Sir." He gestured to Scott turning as he did looking over his left shoulder and then back to us. "Sir, you will not believe your eyes!"

Through the restaurant came this tall dark lady of beauty.

"So, do I look okay? I have not dressed up for ages." Romana announced as she elegantly walked towards us.

Scott looked at me and raised his eyebrows and replied, "I think it's fair to say that for a woman who hasn't dressed up for ages, you've done a pretty good job! You look stunning."

"Well thank you, sir," she said with a blush.

The early diners turned to look for themselves in amazement at this radiant woman. She stepped towards me and pecked me softly on the cheek.

I whispered in her ear, "Your Mama and Papa would be really proud of you, you look so beautiful."

She waited momentarily for Scott. Then she stood between the pair of us and linked her arms into ours.

"Enjoy! Enjoy!" shouted Enrico. "Don't worry about a thing, Maria will keep everything in line I promise, now go, have fun."

The jazz could be heard clearly as we pulled up in Scott's rented jeep.

"You were right; this sounds like real ol' trad'. Now, I know it may seem silly, but what do you want to drink?" I asked.

"Uncle Joe, let's at least get inside!" came their answer.

"Oh! It's alright for you but I probably won't hear a damn thing anyone is saying in there. So what do you want to drink?"

We walked the short distance and entered the hopping and buzzing, almost throbbing, mêlée. I strode up to the bar whilst Romana and Scott found a table. Romana certainly looked radiant as she glided across the dance floor towards a table near to its edge. I must say I felt a little un-comfy. I was definitely the odd one out. But through my eyes I was still of that age. My mind was there, moving and jiving to the music, but I guess my legs were not. I woke again from my 'day dream'. This was becoming a bit of a habit of lately, this daydreaming.

Conversation was sparse really, due mainly to the volume of the band. But, the music was something else. Oh the music. I was in my element. Jazz from that time when I first came here helped fuel those memories. Have you ever looked around a room and thought, I'm towards the end of my short life? I say 'short'. As a man of twenty-two when I came here, life was never going to end. I would party every night till dawn.

I leant across the table.

"Romana," I virtually shouted. "Promise an old man something. Enjoy every moment and never forget it!"

"You're a sentimental old fool. You'll outlive all of us," came her reply. "Remember, Mum always said you were the ultimate survivor!"

She reached over the table and squeezed my hand in a reassuring sort of way.

"Come on! I won't take no for an answer, let's dance!"

"Well he knows I've got a bad leg, so he's not asking me!" I blurted.

Scott moved behind Romana's chair and pulled it out a little to assist her. Out-stretching his hand they moved on to the dance floor.

I watched intently. I hoped that this new found relationship would finish with a happy ending. But, little did they know, a lot of water would have to pass under a very big bridge before any ending would be reached, happy or otherwise.

Looking around the room again I noticed many people from many places. All with a story to tell, but none I fancied as complex as Scott and Romana were to about find out. Or should they? I wrestled with my conscience momentarily. Oh, tomorrow. I'll work this one out tomorrow. But then, as Romana had reminded me only today, I have a habit setting problems aside!

A tap on the shoulder made me jump I was so lost in the ambience. It was Sam from the hotel bar.

"I thought it was you! I didn't think you went anywhere except the Los Santos Hotel."

I stood up to greet him. "Good to see you, Sam, take a seat. I'm here because of Romana, you know, from the Pantry by the harbour? It's all her doing."

"Oh I don't normally sit, Joe, you know me, normally the other side of the bar. Oh, the young American. He was in the Kumota last night wasn't he? Talking to you as I recall, even bought you a drink. Sure I know Romana. Everyone around here knows Romana. She serves up the best seafood that this coast can offer. I even say the best for one hundred miles along the coast. You should get out more you know."

"Perhaps you're right," I replied, adding, "Anyway, I didn't know you came here either."

"Oh it's one of my very few nights off. This music helps my soul. I can relax, I can exercise and I can dream to it."

"Dream to it?" I questioned.

"Yes, dream to it. You know, recollect the days when we were young. Life was less complicated and less busy."

"Sam, my friend, you are a man after my own heart. We have much to talk about, or I should say SHOUT!"

I stood up and gestured to him to follow me. We made our

way outside on to the veranda, sitting at a table overlooking the street. "That's better, why does the music have to be so loud that you can't hear yourself think let alone talk to one another?" I said to him.

We reminisced about the original music artists whose 'hits' the band thundered out. Their renditions did them justice. Standards in any kind of music are timeless. They evoke a mood that encompasses not just the sound, but also the sights and even smells of that time. The spilled beer, bourbon (my favourite) and cigar smoke. Sam and I talked and had a few drinks along the way. I was surprised how he kept pace with me. I glanced back into the dance floor area where Scott and Romana had started talking to other couples who were standing on the other side of the stage. They looked good together. I thought how this happiness might be shattered but deep down I hoped for once I would be wrong. Sam offered me a lift home. It was about eleven thirty and I accepted his offer.

"I'll let the young'ens know."

I made my way through the crowd. "Romana, you know Sam from the Los Santos Hotel? He's offered me a ride home. I'm goin' to take him up on it. Have fun; I'll speak to you tomorrow, promise. Say goodnight to Scott for me. I'll come to the restaurant around lunchtime if that's okay? I won't eat, though. What you gave me today will last a week! Bye, see you tomorrow and you look beautiful, darling." I pecked her on the cheek and made my way back towards Sam.

Despite the volume outside when we had arrived, the sound of the band was welcomingly now quieter on the ear. The warm evening breeze we had every night was refreshingly cool in comparison to the minute by minute increasing heat wave that was the Catfish and Shark.

Sam and I jumped aboard his old battered jeep. This was no Japanese rental vehicle for the tourists. This was the real

McCoy jeep. I started to think as we drove off about what I had just said to Romana. I had referred to her as 'darling'. I had never called her darling, even when she was a small girl. Was this a fraudulent slip or a genuinely affectionate quip?

We drove off back around the edge of the harbour. The sound to our ears this time came from the moored boats with their mainsail sheets chinking against the masts. The air was certainly fresh and pleasant as we headed up through the pine-clad hill. Stars could be seen between the branches every now and then. As we emerged from the last of trees, the bay stretched out before us. Although black, it did not look menacing. We didn't talk. It was as if there was an unwritten law telling us both not to. I sensed that Sam, like me, was at peace with the moment. Sam slowed as we reached the level of the beach road. My porch light could be seen a little way ahead, a few hundred yards or so from where we were.

"Do you mind if I take a couple of minutes here?"

Surprised, I answered, "Well, eh, no."

"It may sound stupid, but please. I just want to savour the moment with someone. We are of the same era, you and me, a dying breed, Joe. We have enjoyed, I think, each other's company tonight – men who have seen a good deal of life. I am not a religious man, but someone out there made all this. Whatever comes our way no one man can take that away from us. We have had this moment. I have never, nor will I ever, ask anything of anyone. But please, just take this in. Enjoy the moment."

I held out my hand to shake his. The grip although firm, was almost heart-warming.

"I think after a long, long time, I have just found a friend. Like you, Sam, I am not religious. But God bless you."

We shook hands and turned to look out to the ocean and upwards towards the stars. Half an hour must have passed as we stood there looking outward and upward.

31

An approaching jeep broke our near meditation. Heading towards us with music blaring from its radio, two or three half-drunks clung on to the roll cage at the back. It bumped its way along the beach road nearly colliding with the gates of the Kumota Plaza Hotel as it entered the grounds. We smiled at each other.

"I think the moment has gone, Joe!" Sam quipped. He dropped me back at the bungalow front door. "See you soon again, young sir," Sam said with a slight sarcastic note.

"Sam, I meant what I said back there. Tonight I found a true friend in you. Long may it last?" I nodded my head and winked. "Oh and there's one more thing, Sam. None of my friends call me sir. It's Joe, please."

I turned and walked the steps to my door. I watched the tail lights disappear into the night.

"Come on you, time for bed," I said to myself. "Tomorrow will soon be here."

CHAPTER FOUR

I woke a lot earlier than usual, around 8 am. I guess the events of the night before had played on my subconscious. After showering and shaving I put the coffee on. Unlike other days one cup was enough to get me going. Looking around the house I realised just how untidy it was. I set to, picking up all the newspapers and magazines strewn everywhere. These were all put in the trash. The morning breeze always helped to freshen up the whole house. I couldn't think when I had gotten up so early. Beavering away as I was, the time soon passed. At around eleven a knock at the door and a call saw me welcoming Scott.

"Good mornin' wow! You've been kinda busy!"

"Well, believe it or not I woke early, looked around and thought it's about time I had a good spring clean! I'll have to have words with the staff!"

"You have people come in and clean for you, Joe?"

"Oh I wish," I replied. "The last woman I had come and clean for me ran out of here screaming hysterics in Spanish at me. If I remember it followed one of my then legendary 'sessions'! If you know what I mean."

"Oh, I think I do," said Scott with that wry smirk of his.

"Anyway, what time did you two leave the jazz bar?"

"Around three, we got back to Romana's just after that. Mind you, we talked till half past four. She sure is an interesting lady," enthused Scott. "Anyway, where's your vacuum, Joe? Let's get this place gleaming!"

"Over here by the sofa. It sounds stupid, but I'm sort of

enjoying this. I don't know if recent events have sparked a new perspective for me or what!"

I felt a warm glow inside. A feeling I can genuinely say I had not felt for years. It was a feeling of being part of something, security, and of being wanted. I smiled to myself and lifted out another pile of old newspapers to the back door to add to the other rubbish now mounting up by the trashcan.

"Oh, we must keep an eye on the time," Scott called through the house above the sound of the, by now, almost over-heating vacuum. "I told Romana we'd come around for lunch today. I hope that's okay with you? I said we would call and let her know what time. Hope you don't think it was too presumptuous of me?" asked Scott.

"No, no not at all, that sounds good."

I had made a start on the bedroom. I changed the sheets, pulled down the old curtains and put them in the twin tub machine. Having done one cycle of a wash I decided to leave them soaking in hot water. I also sorted the wardrobes. There were two of them, both full of clothes, which I guess had not seen the light of day for years. Like so many men, I had my firm favourites when it came to clothes.

Scott called through, "That's the bathroom looking a bit fresher. Just vacuum the hall and I reckon we've done."

I came out of my bedroom dragging the cleaner behind me. "Yes, I can honestly say we done real good!" My room was certainly done. Clothes from the wardrobes filed away neatly. Well, when I say neatly, if I didn't recognize any item or couldn't think when I am likely to ever wear it again… I'd dumped it in the trash!

"Job well done," I said, looking around admiringly at Scott and our efforts.

"Heh, Joe where are your curtains?"

"Oh, soaking. I'll sort them tomorrow, I don't think we have time for me to rinse them out now. We must phone down to Romana, it's nearly a quarter to one. I guess we can say we'll be there in half an hour? That should give us time to quickly freshen up, don't you think?"

"Yeah, you go first if you want, Joe. I'll get me a drink if that's okay? You got any lemonade?"

I called from the kitchen, "Lemonade? You should know me well enough by now that lemonade is something I don't have!" I quipped. I walked through to the living room.

"What are you doing?" I asked. A shiver went through me. Scott was closing the door to the other bedroom opposite mine.

"Oh! I'm sorry I was curious as to what was in here. We hadn't cleaned in here had we?" I walked over the short distance of the hallway pushing past Scott and pulling the door to the room. An awkward silence followed momentarily.

"There are somethings which are best not said or even seen, okay?" I said sternly.

"I'm sorry I didn't mean to pry," replied Scott.

"Come on, let's phone Romana and have that lunch," I said walking back towards the living room.

"I'm sorry, Joe. I didn't mean to upset you."

"I know, Scott. Let's just forget it. I'm just a silly old man, with some silly old ideas. Cleaning through the house and throwing out a whole load of rubbish is one thing. But dumping a closet full of memories is quite another believe me. Come on, please let's not let it spoil our time together. Phone Romana, she'll be wondering where we are!"

At one fifteen we pulled up outside the Ocean's Pantry. I was freshly shaven, wore a clean shirt and had even dusted off my trusty old hat. I felt that comforting glow again. Enrico greeted us as he laid up some tables for lunch.

"Hello to you both, sirs. Madam is upstairs. She said for you to go up when you arrived."

We went through the restaurant into the kitchen, which was buzzing with activity. I gestured to Enrico's wife, but she was busy organizing the staff, no doubt preparing another lunchtime extravaganza of colour and taste. Through a door we went into the small courtyard at the back of the restaurant. Steps led up to an ornate wooden door. A small balcony decorated with wrought iron boxes hung from the framework. Red and orange flowers dazzled in the lunchtime sun.

I knocked and pushed the door gently open, calling to Romana. "Hello, anyone in?"

"Si, come on through, Uncle Joe. Scott is with you too, no?"

"Oh yes, I'm here too," called Scott.

"Okay, I've packed us a picnic of salads and local meats. I can't keep serving my guests fish!" Romana jested.

"Just need my keys, and we will go." She glanced around the room, checking all was in order. Sparse but practical was how I guess you would describe the décor. Traditional wooden framed chairs and a heavy table stood in the dining area. Two large, black leather sofas sat almost menacingly either side of the stone fireplace.

Dressed in jeans, a red blouse and a contrasting neck-scarf of white, she looked, as usual, a million dollars.

"Okay, out we go," she said almost ushering us out. "Enrico, any problems – you know where I am. We'll be back by six."

"Madam, just go, enjoy the afternoon, all will be fine." It was now Enrico's turn to usher us out. Enrico enjoyed his time as the boss, on the odd occasions Romana went out.

"If it's okay with you two, I will drive. That way, Scott, you can take in the scenery and you, Uncle Joe, can have a drink if you want!"

"You had better have some lemonade, Romana. Joe is a changed man."

"Since when?" asked Romana.

"Oh, since this morning!" smirked Scott, looking in my direction.

"No need to mock. Come on, I'll tell you all about it as we get going. You said to Enrico to call if there were any problems, yeah? So where are we going?" I asked.

"Sorry, Uncle Joe, I thought I had said. We are heading out to Senior Rodrigo's plantation."

"Oh not Philippe Rodrigo, you don't still talk to him do you, Romana?"

"He's changed. He's mellowed, now he's older. Anyway, you have to admit the western side of the plantation has got fantastic views over the valley below."

"Rodrigo mellowed! Ha, Rodrigo will only mellow when he's left the mortal world. He's a hard man, Romana. Treats people like dirt, he just uses them. I should know, he used me and many others too!"

"Oh, Uncle Joe, please for me, it's arranged now. Scott will love it up there, I know. Anyway, we're not going to see him. I've just asked to picnic in that area for the afternoon, with some friends."

"He'll want something in return. A free meal at the Ocean's Pantry and him with all that wealth. Yeah, that will be it; he was always a mean man!"

"Uncle Joe, that's not fair, and you know it!" snapped Romana.

I shook my head. "Oh you're right I guess. It's just a lot of things went on between me and him a long time ago, and I'll never forgive him."

"Well by the tone of your voice I would never have guessed it," chipped in Scott.

"Scott, I'm sorry I forgot myself. It's just that that man's name makes my blood boil."

"Like I say, who'd have guessed? Look, Romana reckons we won't even see this guy Rodrigo, yeah? Let's just go, I'm dying to see some of this beautiful countryside I've heard so much about." He glanced across the jeep at Romana.

"Drop me here, Romana, I can walk back to the Ocean's Pantry. It's not far, we haven't been gone too long. You both go and pick me up later."

Romana brought the jeep to a screaming halt.

"If you think I'm going to let you out here to walk back to my restaurant to get drunk all afternoon, you have another thing coming!" she said with stern tone in her voice. "Anyway, I have spent all morning making a picnic for three not two. You're coming, like it or lump it. Even if I have to tie you to the jeep! You can't keep running from the past, let alone still live in it. People change, places change and so do times." Romana scolded me as if she were a school matron. Mind, I was acting a bit like a scorned child as I climbed back into the jeep.

"If he shows I'll… I'll make out that your ham sandwiches didn't agree with me and we'll have to go and be on our way. I can't say fairer than that can I?" I looked at Romana. She shrugged her shoulders and smiled as only she could.

"Well, now that's sorted, shall I start the 'sing song' or you, Romana?" Scott joked. In unison they turned to me and laughed out loud.

"Oh go on with you! Let's get going," I said.

"Yeah, I want to see this countryside," added Scott.

Romana put the jeep back into gear and we headed off again, up through the pine forests. Even I reluctantly joined her and Scott, laughing out loud by the time we had travelled two hundred yards. We wound our way through the back streets of the town. They lay deserted and the shutters closed as the afternoon siesta made for a ghost-like atmosphere. A couple of stray dogs trotted away to find some shade from the burning sun. Out of town the pastures were almost non-existent. I often wondered how any cattle or goats ever survived with little or no grass to feed on in the summer. But, just a bit further on, the barren landscape became lush and green. Here the crops were irrigated from the mountain springs, which were constant all year. Oranges and lemons are the all-important crop. The contrast of colour across acres of land was a sight to behold at harvest time. Further on as we ambled up into the foothills, the olive trees hung heavy with their fruit.

Up we climbed through the pine-clad hillside. On the way, glimpses of Rodrigo's house could be seen every now and then through the trees. The house stood majestically, gleaming white, overlooking the valley. The house towered up over three storeys which was by far and away an exception to the rule in these parts. It was built typically of a Spanish Moorish style, with the various colourful creepers clinging to the frontage making almost natural large archways. It was painted in shades of cream and white and topped off with subtle terracotta roof tiles. The back of the house was even more resplendent than the elegant front. The whole length of the ground floor had a nerja which had any number of chairs tables and chaise longue dotted around in the shaded areas of the terrace.

A large terrace adjoined this, jutting out over the gardens that dropped away, blending as if moulded into the far-reaching landscape and views. To one side, broad sweeping steps curved down towards the pool terrace. Both terraces were tiled in a mosaic and the statues seemed to be looking at you from all angles. All in all this little piece of South America had an almost Mediterranean feel about it, Romanesque.

Before long we drove in through the huge wrought iron gates with their intricate swirling patterns. These were bolted firmly to the walls under the archway. Well-manicured lawns and bushes lined the driveway.

Romana had given a running commentary to Scott all the

way along our journey. Not that I had listened, other than catching the odd word now and again.

Men tended the immaculately manicured gardens. We waved to them as they looked up at us. I wondered what their working lives were like compared to the ones I remembered back when I first met Philippe Rodrigo. My thoughts were brought to a halt as Romana steered the jeep off to the left, down on to a bumpy dirt track towards the plantation fields. We passed by some outbuildings, which housed machinery and tools needed to run such a vast swage of land.

A mile or so on we came to a row of tall pine trees. Romana slowed down and pulled the jeep to the left in between two of the huge pines. Getting out we all looked back over the whole length of our journey.

"Oh wow!" exclaimed Scott.

"Come on, you get this blanket. Spread it out in the shade over there. I'll get the hamper. Uncle Joe, will you help me please?"

I looked up at the pines Rodrigo's grandfather had planted. They were meant to represent the columns found in an ancient Greek temple. Well that's what Philippe had told me many a time. The plantation land had been in their family for generations. The family had always seen themselves as what the British call 'landed gentry'. The difference here though, that throughout each generation, education was never a strong point. Just out and out ruthless hard graft along with some dodgy deals had grown the estate's land and wealth to what it is today.

Talking to me in whispers but with gritted teeth, Romana asked, "What is up with you today? All the way here you were twitchy. Scott must have noticed it as well." Just then I heard the engine of a jeep go past the end of the track we had taken.

"See! You are on edge! Why?" Romana exalted, again

through gritted teeth.

"I thought it was Rodrigo coming to sneer. He'll be here, he'll come."

"Why do you say that? What is it with you? Philippe Rodrigo is a kind, generous and warm man. Why are you so against him?"

"A kind, generous and warm man? Not the Philippe Rodrigo I know. He would tread on anyone to make a cent. That's how he's got all of this, and anyone who works for him lives in poverty!"

"Oh, so that's it, is it? You are jealous! Don't tell me. You lost to him playing poker years ago I bet probably with my father? He made it big and you… you!"

"Hey you guys. I know you go back a long way, but can we eat?" Scott had cut in at the right time.

"We'll be right there," called Romana. "We'll talk later or better still tomorrow at my place. Come on, I don't want to spoil this afternoon. Uncle Joe, people change, move on with their lives and learn from their mistakes. You must too. Tomorrow at around eleven, there is much to say."

"I guess you are right," I answered. "Come on let's eat."

We laid out the contents of the hamper. As usual our host had done us proud. There were hams, cheeses and bread. There was also a separate hamper of fruit. They were presented with an almost artistic flair as opposed to just being flung into a basket and it made it look all the more colourful and delicious.

"That's good. The wine is still fairly cold. Uncle Joe, some white wine?"

The afternoon passed happily. We drank a little and ate a lot. I lay against one of the pines, pulled my hat down over my eyes and just took in the stillness. Scott and Romana talked and laughed together. I couldn't hear what they said, but instinct told me they enjoyed each other's company. I must have dozed off for a while. Waking, I felt a little chilly. The sun had swung around to the west dropping as it went. I heard voices. A voice in particular stood out from the others. Lifting my hat and stretching I saw Romana come towards me. "Uncle Joe, nice snooze? We have company."

"There! What did I say, Philippe Rodrigo! Has he come to gloat?"

"Uncle Joe! Enough! For me, be nice. You and I will talk tomorrow. Tell me then, okay? Obviously there is a lot I don't know. But please not now. Not in front of Scott."

I agreed, and with Romana the three of us walked across to his jeep, a very large shiny American jeep. More scandalous deals, I thought. Sat up in the back was the ever-present help that Rodrigo had always had around him. I don't think he had ever gone anywhere without some kind of muscle to back him up.

"Joe, it's so good to see you. God it must be, what, twenty-five years?"

"It's twenty-seven actually."

He was a small man, about five six or seven, quite chubby now in the face. He always was stocky, that hadn't changed. He was almost fat now around the waist. His shock of black hair was shorter than I remembered and his temples were starting to turn grey. He still wore the moustache, like a pencil line above his top lip, waxed on the ends giving it an exaggerated upward lift. His clothes looked timeless. He had on a crisp white shirt open at the neck. The cravat around his neck was a golden yellow. At one time he was renowned for his cravats. It was said that you could tell what kind of mood Rodrigo was in by the colour of them. I don't think there was any real evidence to this claim. In my opinion, he was still a deceitful man even if he were butt naked. The pale lemon chinos with sharply pressed creases to the front complemented his cravat, turned up over light tan Italian leather shoes.

Holding out his hand, I reluctantly shook it. "You're keeping well as ever I see." I tilted my head slightly to one side. Even this comment got my defences up. In my opinion anything Philippe Rodrigo said or did, had an angle, or an alternative motive behind it.

"Romana, darling you are looking as radiant as only you can!" He brushed by me as he spoke again, holding his hands towards Romana. Kissing her on both cheeks he kept hold of her hands, now at arm's length and looked her up and down.

"Oh, you're so like your mother, wouldn't you say so, Joe?" He turned and gave a wry smile and winked. Just as I had thought, the quips were there but just a bit quicker than I had anticipated.

This man truly was a nasty piece of work. Treading on anyone to get what he wanted when he wanted it. I had hoped that maybe with the passing of time he may have mellowed, but this last remark demonstrated that was not the case. Perhaps it was just me, could it be that he had softened with his old enemies? Even forgiven them or they had passed away so were no longer a threat to his ways? I was still around even after twenty-seven years. Sure, we had not crossed paths during that time, but today's chance meeting had stirred something of the old Rodrigo that I once knew.

"Are you going to introduce me to this young man then?" He strode towards Scott.

"Oh forgive me, Philippe. This is Scott Kowlowski. Scott is from America, he is my cousin, and he's here on a short holiday." Rodrigo's face glowed with an almost delight.

"America. Oh, I love America." They shook hands.

"You have been to the US, Senor Rodrigo?"

"Please call me Philippe as all my friends do. Yes, I have been on a couple of occasions, but not for some time. It was when the business needed some kind of boost financially to help expand it; I went to look for some new investment opportunities."

All the time he spoke he would give a glance at me. I couldn't help but think he was either seeking my approval or vying me to say something to contradict what he was actually saying. Either way, I didn't like his attitude. He may have aged and look changed, but his way of dealing with and manipulating people obviously had not.

"Tell me, Scott, when do you return the US?"

"I go back in a week or so, this was only a short break. But I have learned so much in such a short space of time and I shall definitely be coming back, hopefully for a much longer time as well."

"Oh good, I will look forward to that." Rodrigo had an expression of thought on his face. What he conjuring up now I wondered? "Dinner. What was I thinking; you must all come to dinner. Shall we say tomorrow night, around eight? We can all talk more then."

We were all taken aback a bit by his almost abrupt request.

"Romana, won't you find it hard to get cover in the restaurant for an evening? You know it was difficult to have lunch here today with us," I quickly responded, breaking the uncomfortable silence.

"Nonsense, nonsense," cut in Rodrigo. "You will be telling me you need to stay in and wash your hair, old man! That chap you have down there, whatever his name is, it escapes me just now. He will cover for you. It will do him good to run it of a night anyway. Give him some needy experience I'm sure. I'll send a car for seven thirty to the restaurant; it can pick all three of you up from there. I must go now, much to do, but I look forward to seeing you all again –especially you, Romana. Till tomorrow then. Adios." With that he again brushed by me turning his head as he went. "Oh, Joe, don't worry about dressing for dinner, it will be a casual affair." With that he got in his jeep and raced away.

We all stood motionless as we watched the dust settle again from the jeep.

"Well, I guess from that we all know what we're doing tomorrow night. Or at least if we don't necessarily know what, we sure as hell know where we'll be tomorrow night!" exclaimed Scott.

"Yes, it seemed a bit direct didn't it? Quite different to when I have met him before over the years I have known him," Romana remarked.

"What did I say, Romana? Once a dirty dog always a dirty dog! I can read him like a book. Ah Scott, he's from the US, going back soon, but returning shortly. He's already hatching a plan mark my words."

Scott's eyes lit up like fireworks when he heard that.

"Oh Uncle Joe, your imagination will get the better of you one of these days," Romana uttered.

"I don't like to take sides, Romana, but I did get the same kinda feeling myself," said Scott, agreeing with me.

We decided to pack up our picnic things and made our way back down through the plantation, heading back to the harbour. The sun was still fairly high as it was only around four thirty. The quay was busy as it usually was at this time with the few tourists getting off the fishing boats, returning from their day out, no doubt fishing for marlin. The bigger fish always drew a crowd, even getting the locals looking at the best catch.

Pulling up outside the Ocean's Pantry we heard the calling out 'hellos' of the skippers from the boats. They were all keen to impress Romana. Remember, she was their biggest customer. She and her staff would turn large chunks of fish meat into a gastronomic delight. Smiling and waving at them all she made each man feel welcome and most important that they should know the proprietor of the best fish restaurant for miles in either direction of this coastline. She made several comments about their day's fishing expedition. Had Sergio been out beyond the reef today as looked a little breezy? Had Jose caught any more congers? She said she was still trying to think of a recipe to use the last catch of his.

The whole quay laughed as the friendly banter switched from one side to the other. This was Romana at her best. She was not just a good cook, a good businesswoman; she could hold an audience and command respect. She was a people person and people loved her for it.

"Do you want a small beer to clear the dust, Uncle Joe?"

"Ah yes, that would be good. What needs to be done around here before you open up again for the evening, then?"

"Are you offering?"

"Well I did say if you remember that I was a changed man."

"I'll get you that beer and think about it. Scott, a beer for you as well?" Romana went through to the bar inside. Scott and I sat at the table just around the corner in the shade. Romana came through with a tray of bottled beer, followed by Enrico.

"Hello how was your picnic?" Enrico enthused.

"Oh, fantastic and also different," I said.

"What Uncle Joe means is that we had a visit from Philippe Rodrigo. He has invited us three to dinner tomorrow night. Will you and Maria be okay to run the Pantry? We were sort of pushed into accepting his invitation."

"It's a no problem. You go, enjoy. Maria and I will be fine. You should go out more times. You are young; enjoy how you say, more times go out. Maria and me, we are old. We just enjoy being 'ere." With that a loud shout in Spanish came from inside the bar aimed at Enrico

Maria came storming through the open doors to where we were sitting. She turned a bright colour of red almost matching the slow sinking sun. "Oh! Mama Mia!" she cried, then started to laugh out loud with us. She hadn't realised Romana was back and that Enrico had sneaked in for a quick beer before laying up the tables for the evening's dinner.

"Maria, get a glass and join us. Enjoy," said Romana. They talked at what seemed one hundred miles an hour to each other in Spanish, pausing only to laugh. Sometimes they would both look at either Scott or Enrico and then laugh. But when they looked at Scott, Maria had a gaze of contentment, looking at a fine young man in her opinion. Whereas Romana, she looked at Scott with almost a glint of love. The glances at Enrico on the other hand were just born out of laughter. Even my limited grasp of their language told me this. Poor old Enrico. I sat back and listened to the conversation and just savoured the moment. Times like these are all too often just taken for granted by people. I have learned over the years to think about moments like this. It can sometimes be seen as ignorant because I don't necessarily join in with the conversation for a period of time. But really I am just simply relishing the moment.

"Uncle Joe, you okay?" asked Romana.

"Yeah, I'm fine, couldn't be better. As I was saying earlier, what needs doing before tonight?"

"Are you trying to earn your keep or something? You don't have to work for your supper while I'm around here, you silly old man."

"Like I say, I'm a changed man. Just recently I have realised I need to get up and do something to occupy my time once more. I can still fit in a good drink every now and again if I want, just try not to do it quite as often as I have done in the past that's all."

"I don't think you are cut out for what we call 'front of house' work, Uncle Joe. But we always have things to do around the place like fixing things, maintenance I guess. You used to do it for Mom and Dad when I was growing up. So why not start over and do the same for me? I can't pay much but as you know I can feed you," she said, smiling. I held out my hand and took off my old hat. "Uncle Joe, I don't mind shaking your hand as long as you don't 'spit' on it!" We all laughed, even Maria understood Romana's joke. I stood and hugged her and whispered my thank you to her.

"A toast is in order!" Scott called out. "To Joe and his new house, new job and his new life. To Joe!"

"I too wish to make a toast. Quite simply, to my new family, of friends that is."

Our sentimental merriment was short lived by a large man holding at, arm's length, a hand full of small anchovy. Almost shouting, the gentleman asked, "Can you cook these for me? The man on the boat said you would do a real good job of cooking these here fish. Is that right? I don't mind paying, neither!"

"I take it from your accent you must be from the Midwest?"

"Hell yeah! Are you from the US, son? Ain't sure about this 'ere Spanish lingo, ya know."

"Yeah, it can be a bit of a problem for them understanding some of us good ol' boys!" Scott mocked.

Our new friend wasn't quite sure what was being said and looked a little puzzled at Scott. We all knew though and again spontaneously laughed in unison. Romana got up out of her chair and approached the man.

"Sir, these are fine fish. Who did you sail with today?"

"I think the skipper's name is Sergio, ma'am."

"Did you catch these out near the reef? Because it's only ever Sergio's boat that can catch these fine fish." Scott choked on his beer at this last remark. "What time would you like to dine with us tonight, sir?"

Slightly bemused by now, the gentleman turned to ask his wife. She was not so elegantly dressed in striped orange shorts and a green-hooped T-shirt. Her hair was definitely wind-swept from their day's activities.

"Sugar, what time would like to eat tonight? This lady would like to know so she can prepare our catch."

"By the time I get myself presentable I reckon it'll be around eight!"

At this point her heel caught on the cobble of the quay-side. The more she struggled the worse it got. Her companion meanwhile tried to assist in vain. Eventually her heel broke clean away from her shoe.

"Uncle Joe, I think that is your first 'fixing job', doesn't you knows?" Again Romana was as a quick as a flash with her sense of humour. "Leave the shoes and the fish, senor, tonight you will eat well, and you, madam, will walk away in those shoes. We look forward to seeing you both later."

"Well if that's okay with you. We'll be around for a drink at eight and eat if we may at eight thirtyish. Oh and I'm Jerry, Jerry Colbert and this here is my wife, Thelma, but we all call her Ma. That's me and the kids that is."

We all introduced ourselves and then Jerry and Thelma, who was now wearing a pair of Romana's shoes, made their way back towards the hotel. Smiling, Romana passed me the shoes. "C'mon, let's take a look in the storeroom out back. I'm sure there are lots of tools in there."

We walked through the kitchen into the old storeroom. Adjacent to this room was an entrance doorway to an outbuilding. I used to use this as a workshop with Bob. I hadn't been in there for years. It was just as I had remembered it, a bit dusty and there were cobwebs everywhere. But nothing that a good clean up wouldn't sort out.

When Bob had gone my drinking had become heavier and I lost interest in a lot of things. At the time I remember thinking that I was the one who should have been taken. Unlike Bob, I had no family to leave behind. Life at that time seemed so unjust. I shook my head in a knowingly sort of a way.

"I'll fix the shoes now, and then if it's okay with you, tomorrow around nine I'll be back to make a start on this place!" I said looking around the workshop.

"Could you make it more around ten, Uncle Joe? Bear in mind by the time I finish here tonight I won't get to bed before two."

"Ten thirty it is then, boss. You can have a lie in!" I joked. "Right, that's settled I'll do these shoes now and then tomorrow morning clean up here. If you can get Enrico to make a list of things to do I can start on anything small in the afternoon?"

"Uncle Joe, I am so pleased for you. You make me feel so happy. I feel inside like it was when Papa and Mom were here. You and Papa would be in here making noises, banging, crashing, grinding things and laughing. Oh how you both would laugh. Mom always said to me no wonder there was always jobs needed to be done around here, 'those two are like a couple of school boys messing around'!"

"I haven't felt this happy for such a long time. But, Romana, we must talk, just you and me, soon. There are things I need to share with you."

"Philippe Rodrigo you mean?"

"Well, yes, he will be some of what I want to say. I must say I don't like the thought of what he might have in store for us tomorrow night. But, the time has come to tell you so much more about me. Now is not that time. Tomorrow I will come by at ten thirty, clean up here then we will talk, upstairs, if that is okay?"

"You sound serious. I hope I am not going to lose this happy feeling?" A concerned expression came over her face.

"Oh please, no, don't worry. It's just to talk. I feel I need to tell you one or two things, that's all."

Romana tilted her head slightly to one side. "Okay we'll do that. Now, now I must get to work on that fine catch of our American friend. You must repair his darling wife's shoes. I'll leave you to it."

"Hey, Romana, don't worry, what I have to tell you is for the good. But what I will say is, let's look forward, all of us. You, me and Scott, oh and not forgetting Enrico and Maria, bless them."

Her face lost that concerned look and began to glow again. "Agreed, let's look forward. Now, I really must do something with these fish!"

She went back through to the kitchen. I set about looking for the necessary bits and bobs to repair the broken shoe heel. The shoes readily repaired I took them back into the kitchen and gave them to Enrico.

"How's those fish coming on then?" I quipped.

"Oh, pretty good. I have marinated them in one of my secret recipes. The shoes are okay, yes?" asked Romana.

"Yeah, good as new I guess. I'm going to head back home, it's been a long day."

"Stay. Eat here with Scott and me."

"No, you don't want me hanging around. I'll see you tomorrow, around ten thirty."

Remembering what we were to talk about, Romana's face momentarily relaxed from her usually pleasing expression. "Okay, see you in the morning then. How will you get home? Scott brought you here didn't he?"

"I'll wander over to see if old Sam is about. It's his night off. We'll have a couple of drinks together and he'll run me back. It's on his way home. See you." I pecked her on the cheek and headed out through the restaurant.

Sure enough Sam was sat at the bar of the Catfish and Shark. "Evening, Sam, you want the same again?"

We sat and talked. I told him of the day's events, especially of my concerns surrounding tomorrow night's dinner at the Rodrigo plantation.

"Tell me, Joe, are you going to explain to Romana why you

dislike Rodrigo so much?"

Sam was one of the few people left who had been around long enough to know what had gone on before. Some say the 'good old days', but when I look back I'm not so sure.

"Yes, I've decided to tell her everything at her place tomorrow morning. I can't say I'm looking forward to it. I don't really know where to start. It's something maybe I should have done long ago. But, now with this young man Scott, her cousin, turning up, well maybe the time is right!"

"Whatever the outcome, I wish you well. I'm sure it's for the best. She has a right to know, and she can do as only she sees fit. You want another beer or shall we make a move home?"

"Looking at the time I'll take you up on that ride home."

We finished our beers and went out to Sam's jeep. I kept wondering how I was going to start my conversation with Romana in the morning. Straight in I suppose. How could anyone tell someone who had for years thought of them as just a friend to the family, whilst growing up, was in fact related? As much as I pondered and thought, I couldn't see any other way than to just come straight to the point and tell her. Romana's was my daughter.

As we rode home along the beach road nothing was said. Sam brought the jeep to a stop outside my house.

"Bear in mind things, people and circumstances have all changed during Romana's life time. You must make her understand that. At that time when it happened, you did what you thought was the right thing. The best thing for her, no one else, and it's the same now as it was then. You only ever want what is the best for her."

"Sam, you are a profound man, with profound thoughts. You're wasted as a barman."

"Good night, Joe, sleep well." He smiled and drove off down the dusty trail towards his house.

CHAPTER FIVE

After what was a restless night I got up at around eight thirty. I went to bed thinking of the coming morning and how best to start the conversation. Waking several times it played on my mind, each time never reaching the end of the story. Showered and shaved with a couple of coffees inside me I felt better and more confident by a long chalk.

I parked my jeep opposite the Ocean's Pantry. Romana was laying up some tables. A couple of regulars, fishermen, were having coffee.

"No rest for the wicked then? What time did you finish last night?" I said almost nervously. I sensed that there was an atmosphere.

"Two, same as usual," Romana responded. This morning's talk was obviously foremost on her mind as well. But maybe she was short through nervousness. Nervous of not knowing what it exactly was I was going to say. I followed her through the courtyard and up the stairs to her apartment.

"Window boxes are looking really colourful," I said this time with a quiver in my voice.

She closed the door behind me. "I don't know what this is about but I feel so anxious and I hardly slept. I was up at seven. I had to get busy. I kept telling myself, 'Uncle Joe, he won't make me unhappy. Not my uncle Joe'. Tell me you won't. I just feel there is something, but I don't know what."

"Oh Romana, I hope what I have to say won't make you unhappy. But what I do say to you is long overdue. Somehow things have changed. Long ago, in my dreams I was going to tell you but in reality it never seemed right. I think now the time is right. How can I not tell you something that is so important to us both?

"I will try to explain as best I can with a memory not as good as it used to be. There are some things that in our lives we never forget and what I am going to tell you now is one of those things that is etched on to my memory forever."

And so I began. "I drank! No big secret there I hear you say. But it is why I started to drink. I never wanted to say goodbye to you, or to your mom. My thoughts and plans never lived up to my dreams, or are it the other way around? I felt at one time I was going insane but it was just the booze. Thank God for your mom and papa. They pulled me, even dragged me, through that hell."

"What are you trying to say, Uncle Joe?"

"There is no easy way to tell you. No gentle way to ease into conversation. Okay, I'm going to just blurt it out and then, then I'll explain everything to you. But please, please promise me you won't be mad. Oh that's a stupid thing to say, you're bound to be mad."

I looked at her, until now my gaze had been around the room, even looking down at the floor. It was only now that I was consciously looking at her. She looked pensive and rightly so. I wasn't making a very good job of this, I thought to myself.

I took a huge gasp of air. "Romana," I paused.

"Just tell me please, you've started, please just tell me."

"Romana, darling I'm your father. There I've said it!"

"I knew it, I knew it! I just felt something inside me since you said last night, I knew!"

"And?" I asked gingerly.

"Momma said something to me when I was about six or seven. I was dressed up to go to a party I think. She took a picture of me, on this old camera." She held up an old box camera from the solid dresser. "I remember her saying something like, 'If only your papa could see you now'. But what I didn't understand was that Papa was holding me on his hip for the picture. She meant you, didn't she?"

"I guess. When you were six or seven though, I was in no fit state for any small children to see. There I was un-shaven, un-washed, my same old clothes and me. Not to mention always reeking of drink. But your mom and papa stood by me through all of that time.

"I couldn't see anything for its beauty or worth back then. Only recently have I truly seen things for their real value and beauty. My life has passed me by through the bottom of a glass, but no more. I want to relish every minute of all my lasting days." Continuing, I watch Romana listening with such attentiveness.

"Oh Romana, Romana, where do I start? Rodrigo, he is in a way, or was, the main cause. He may forgive or just conveniently forget, but I don't and never will! Your real mother was a young woman of twenty-three when I first met her. I'd been here a year or so. There was the odd glance across the street or in the bar of Bob and Louise's hotel. Your mom introduced me to her. Juanita was her name. I later found out she had said to Louise she wanted to get to know me but was a bit shy. She was a private lady. The only time she would talk freely was to people she trusted. Never full-on like so many people."

Romana sat quietly as I recollected that time. I felt the mood in the room change. It was calmer now. I felt more at ease. A weight was slowly being lifted. Feeling this I asked Romana, "Are you okay with this?"

"Talk, Uncle Joe, just talk. I need and want to know. What did she look like?"

"Romana when you look in the mirror you look at your mother. She looked as you do in every way. She had long jet-black hair down to just above her waist as you do. And deep green eyes just like yours. You are around the same height as well."

I walked across to the window and looked out to the harbour. People were going about their own everyday lives, caught up in their own world, and here was me, re-living mine and someone I felt so much for.

"Rodrigo, where does he fit into all of this?"

"Your mom worked for him in his shipping office, down on the quayside. Her desk was by the third window, on the left up there." I nodded my head in the direction of the buildings at the far end of the headland which used to be the busy with ships from all over.

"I could never prove it, back then or now. She knew too much about Rodrigo's empire. The sort of the things he was shipping. In his opinion she had been there too long and had to go. Bear in mind back then, the police were, shall we say, financed by Rodrigo. He could do anything he wanted around this area and he took full advantage of the situation. As time has gone by though, he's had to clean up his act. Changes of government and tighter regulations with the police have put more pressure on the likes of the Rodrigos of this country.

Juanita and I didn't get the chance to marry, but she fell pregnant with you after eighteen months of us first meeting. We had so many plans, so many dreams. We would sit on my veranda most nights watching the sun set and talk about everything and then again, nothing. We were just living for each other, no one else figured in our lives, just us two, soon to be three. There was many a morning when we would also wake and watch the sun rise."

I swallowed hard. "But one man took that from me. Philippe Rodrigo!" I swallowed again.

"I remember one morning I drove like a madman from

my bungalow down to the shipping office to get her to work on time. We'd watched the sun rise. I made some coffee, we sat together on that old hammock I have on the veranda. I went to get a blanket off the bed to wrap around us. It was a bit chilly at that time of day. There was no real warmth from the sun's rays.

"I turned around; Juanita was standing in the doorway of the bedroom. She said nothing, took my hand and walked back towards the bed. We made love. We said nothing. We had made love before, but those times were... I'm sorry, I must be embarrassing you?"

"No please, tell me." Romana had moved beside me at the window. So caught up in my thoughts I had not heard her approach. She smiled and held out her hand to mine.

"Please, go on."

I shook my head and gathered my thoughts once more. We had made love before many times, but that was more lust for each other than love. We would talk, we would giggle, and those times were for physical pleasure. This time it was cherished and loved. It was as if we had at that moment in time a sixth sense between us."

I turned from looking out of the window and looked at Romana. Her eyes were glistening with tears.

"You were the love we shared on that morning." A broad smile enveloped her face and she walked towards me.

"Hold me," she gently asked. I held her for the first time as a father holds his newborn child, with a look of pride and wonderment. I had never been able to hold her like this before. Not a close embrace. Yes, I'd embraced her before at parties or Christmas. But that was always as 'good old Uncle Joe' not as her father. She let go of me and moved back to the chair.

"You said Rodrigo was the cause of her going, I don't want to say her death. What do you mean?"

"She worked in his office. She was responsible for invoicing and chasing up non-payments of goods he had supplied. Originally the goods were bananas from the plantation or timber from high up in the forest region. Rodrigo has land up that way. Vast areas I believe. Oh, and of course olives and his vineyards. One day I remember Juanita telling me she was introduced to some Americans he'd met in the hotel bar. They became regular visitors to the office. For two or three months they came in a couple of days every month. After that she didn't see them. But the invoices highlighted large sums of cash coming in from the States. Amounts of money that were far higher than the average price of bananas or olives. In any case nobody gets paid cash for bananas!

"That morning, when I raced her to the office, she had told me the night before that she was worried it was drugs. She had confronted Rodrigo about it, saying if it was she would leave his office. She didn't want anything to do with drugs. Drugs had been the downfall within her family. Then, like now, the farmers and fishermen would take drugs to ease their day to day worries. She had, on the other hand, risen above the poverty her father had imposed on their family due to his own habit. She had done well at school, got an education and a job. Even a job working for Rodrigo was a good job back then.

"Once she had confronted him about drugs, Rodrigo's attitude towards her changed. His mood and temper got worse. There was many a time when she said she was ready to quit. But of course, jobs like hers were hard to find around here.

Anyway, what made it worse was she was pregnant. We both said it was that whimsical night we had shared. Juanita did not like being pregnant, or rather the duration of pregnancy, as she was just impatient to have the baby.

"The coming months became hard for her – what with slowing down because she had to and Rodrigo putting more pressure on her. She finished work when she was seven and a half months' pregnant. I wanted her to finish sooner because of Rodrigo's demanding ways, but she was a determined woman, just like you. No one, not even Rodrigo, was going to get the better of her."

"What I don't understand, if you are my father and Juanita was my mother, where does my mom and papa fit in? And I have to say, they will always be my mom and papa!" Romana cut in.

"Oh without a doubt." I tried to reassure her. "Let me explain. She had finished work for Rodrigo and moved into the hotel with your mom and papa. They were so supportive to both of us. Your mom was like a sister to Juanita. Remember, there were no other kids in their lives. Scott and his sister, Bob's niece and nephew, were thousands of miles away in the States. Also, Bob and his brother were worlds apart.

"It was around that time that Louise learned she couldn't have children. Anyway, Rodrigo came into the bar demanding to see Juanita. He was pretty annoyed and raised his voice causing a scene. As usual then and now he had his 'heavies' in tow to back him up. Typical little bull terrier is our Senor Rodrigo. Juanita came down from her room. He pulled her by the arm shouting that she had some unfinished business to attend to. I don't know, the books didn't balance or something. I lurched at him, telling him to get off her. Needless to say his henchmen intervened. Next thing I know I'm picking myself up off the floor. Bob had a go but he was stopped in his tracks by one of them unclipping the safety clip on his pistol. I can still see the hatred in his eyes as he shouted that he would bring her back if and when his books were sorted.

"I drove like a maniac down to the shipping office with Bob. We couldn't get near because of Rodrigo's men. We caught glimpses of him and Juanita now and again at her desk. She had her back to us but was sometimes obscured by one of his gorillas blocking our view. Rodrigo was leant over the table towards her, remonstrating. He lost it. He started shaking her.

"That was enough for Bob and me. We said nothing, looked at each other and ran headlong towards the main door. I don't remember seeing anyone. We were in and up those stairs as quick as a flash. Bob burst the door open and knocked the big guy clean off his feet. He quickly put paid to the other two who were still alarmed at the speed at which we had come in. Rodrigo was on the other side of the office, his back to an open door that led to another stairway down to the roadway into the quayside docks area. Motionless, he was staring down at the floor. I went for him. I only hit him once and he fell. I went to kick him while he was on the floor, but Bob grabbed me and shouted for me to leave him.

"I then looked around, looking for Juanita. I couldn't see her in the office. Then, as if a massive sickness had hit me smack between my eyes and gripped my stomach at the same time, I ran towards the open doorway above the stairway. Despite Bob's earlier effort to stop me from kicking Rodrigo before, I swung around and caught him hard and square in his stomach with my right boot just as he was slumbering up off the floor. There, on the ground at the foot of the stairs was Juanita.

"Without a split second's hesitation I was down at the bottom of the flight of stairs cradling her in my arms. She was bleeding around the nose and mouth, her body twisted awkwardly with one of her legs underneath her. Although semi-conscious we picked her up and shouted to someone to get a car or truck to help us take her to a doctor. There was a small crowd of men who had gathered. Many men would have no doubt liked to have been of assistance had they known what was happening to Juanita. Man on man was not to be condoned in these parts but even in this male dominant place that was reasonably accepted. But no man worth his salt would ever consider hitting a woman.

"Rodrigo and his henchmen ran past us. He was getting into a car shouting something like, "Let that be a lesson to you, Bampton. Let that be a lesson to you all!" The car screamed away from the quayside. I didn't see Rodrigo for some months after that day, come to that, no-one did. He kept a very low profile. The police were not much better either. Despite our efforts none of the men Rodrigo had there that day were brought to justice.

"I don't remember much else. We got her back to the hotel and got the doctor. All the commotion had caused the baby to come a bit sooner than expected. You were delivered a short while later. Louise put you into Juanita's arms. She kissed your forehead, looked around the room, smiled to everyone and mouthed, "I love you, God bless." Then she closed her eyes and slipped away. I shall never forget that night and never, ever forgive that man. If indeed you can call him a man!"

Sitting down, Romana quietly and slowly moved her hands up to her face in a thoughtful manner. She stroked her cheek. I'd seen this look before. Meanwhile, I just stood in the middle of the room, silent. I tuned in, momentarily to the usual bustle of outside but that was short lived as Romana got up and spoke.

"Right then, it's settled! We go to dinner as arranged and we say nothing to Senor Rodrigo. Let's at least have the main course before we say anything. I was never one much for dessert!"

"And Scott? Shall we tell him?" I asked. "He has every right to know. In any case, we may need his support there tonight."

"Yes. I think you are right. Where is Scott just now, still at

61

the Los Santos Hotel?"

"I guess so; let's find him."

Romana got straight up, a determined look on her face and headed for the door.

We both crossed the road to my jeep. I swung it around on the quayside nearly knocking over some poor bystander looking at the freshly caught fish being landed from the trawlers.

"Hey! What's your rush, buddy?"

The tyres squealed on the tarmac, my vision seemed tunnel-like as I was only focused on getting to the hotel and seeing Scott. It was only a short drive from the quay into the square in the middle of town where the hotel was. Bringing the jeep to a screeching halt more pedestrians jumped as Romana and I swiftly entered the hotel lobby.

There was a young lad behind the desk, eighteen or nineteen years old. He looked slightly alarmed as Romana abruptly asked for Scott.

"He's over here," said Scott. He was sitting in the front window on a large high-backed chair holding a coffee in one hand and a newspaper in the other.

"Is there a fire somewhere? Cos you guys came down the street as if there was!" The position of the chair faced back looking in the direction of the quay.

"Please, can we have some more coffee, Pedro," Scott asked the young lad. "Now, what's the problem?"

We waited for Pedro to bring the coffee before I started to repeat my previous conversation with Romana. Pedro returned to behind the desk and Romana and I explained to Scott the story from beginning to end.

"Well I gotta say that's one hell of a story. Firstly you two are father and daughter. How do you both feel about that? Never mind all this other stuff. That kinda falls by the wayside a bit doesn't it?" asked Scott.

Romana and I just looked at each other. I think in the whirlwind of events and stories we had discussed this morning the real important thing here had almost been brushed aside, so much was our need to get revenge with Rodrigo. Maybe our true thoughts and realization about our relationship were there, but our unsaid need to seek justice against Rodrigo meant we had overlooked this fact. But no, I am convinced that both our minds had similar thoughts of this new found love running through them. Romana held out her hand and squeezed mine. I firmly but gently responded. Smiling, we knew there was more to say, just not at this moment in time.

"So what's next then?" asked Scott quietly but firmly. "It seems you both want some kind of revenge by the sound of your tone." He looked thoughtful for a moment, refilled his cup from the coffee pot, sat back again in his chair. "Well, I guess you'd better count me in. But, and I do mean 'but', is there a plan?" Scott added.

"No plan as yet. But revenge, yes, and I think I speak for Romana as well as myself." I glanced across at her and she nodded.

"Yes, revenge is the only choice I have."

"C'mon, finish your coffee. Let's talk about this away from everyone. This will be our one and only chance at getting justice from the murderous Senor Rodrigo. If nothing else he will pay for his underhand dealings and bullyboy regime over the past twenty or so years. It may also put a stop to any shenanigans he may be involved in just now as well."

We drank up and quietly left the hotel, nodding at young Pedro as we went. He smiled slightly, almost nervously, probably still considering the reason behind our swift arrival.

We climbed into the jeep in silence. I drove back towards the quay, turning right towards the headland road. I had a place in mind as being the perfect spot to discuss our thoughts and plans. I just caught sight of Romana and Scott smiling at each other in a knowing sort of way as I glanced in the rear view mirror.

Arriving back at my bungalow I walked straight into the kitchen to make some fresh coffee leaving the two of them to contemplate the next move.

"Open up the shutters please. I'll bring the coffee out on to the veranda." A few minutes later I brought out the tray with the freshly brewed coffee. Sitting together on my swinging hammock, almost like two young teenagers, Scott and Romana gently rocked back and forth. Placing the tray down, Romana offered to be mother. I sat back in my favourite chair looking up the beach off the end of the headland, seeing the surfers catching the waves.

Turning to look at Scott I started to consider there might be a connection between Scott and Rodrigo. This link might enable us to extract information, although quite what, I did not know.

"Scott, I noticed when you were first introduced to Rodrigo his eyes lit when he realised you were American. I think we need to play on that reaction if that's okay with you. When I look back to that fateful time there were always the trips to the States. Plus, there was a couple of Americans hanging out with him back then.

"Do you think these guys were kinda heavies?" Scott questioned.

"Heavies, what do you mean heavies?" Romana asked.

I was quick to answer her. My recollections were now entering my head thick and fast. "You know, Mafia, back then they operated a lot around here. Yes I'm sure there was a reason the Americans were hanging around. Bob and I often talked about the possibility of them being involved. Mind you, the more I think about it, the more I remember how there were all sorts coming out of the woodwork.

Yeah, there were Italians and even Germans. They raised a few eyebrows round here, I tell you. But they never stayed around for long, some for a couple of days, a week maybe. Then they would be gone. Rumour had it some were ex-SS or Nazi leaders. Whenever these characters were in town, so was Rodrigo. Don't know where they stayed though."

"I suspect not in the town," Scott cut in. "Up at Rodrigo's house I bet."

"It's more than likely. Back then his place was absolutely crawling with fellas. You couldn't get within a mile of the plantation let alone get near to the house without being stopped." I continued, "Oddly though, the Americans always stayed at Bob and Louise's hotel. Big tippers, I remember that. They were big drinkers too. The two that I remember most though would only sleep at the hotel, rarely frequenting the bar. They were always at the office or over by the quayside where the ships were docking back then. They were really snappy dressers too. They wore bright coloured shirts and really sharp suits, crisp linen I reckon. That tailored Italian cut of the forties. Ah, what I am saying? You two won't know about the cut of a suit. I remember seeing one of them wearing a shirt and waistcoat without the jacket. I was leaning against the bar as usual at about six o'clock when he came down the stairs from his room. He stood next to me and ordered a coffee. I couldn't help but notice his pocket watch. I had never seen anything like it. It had a gold face, but subtle not garish in any way. I made a comment to him about it. He told me it was eighteen carat gold, 'hunting cased' which he went on to tell me would help to protect it against all sorts of knocks. He then continued to tell me it was also a keyless pocket watch. It was made by A Lange & Sohne, one of the finest German watchmakers. I can't say I had heard of them but he told me with an air of arrogance in his voice. It's funny how you remember little things like that, even after all this time. When they did drink in the bar at the hotel, though, the other guys would seem to be on their best behaviour. I wish I could remember their names."

"Their names may be very important," interrupted Scott. "Try to think of them, Joe. I have some contacts back home in the police who might help us. It's surprising what may be kept on record even after all this time."

"What about me?" Romana asked.

"You will be the distraction we need. If I'm the American connection he might want to do business with me. Joe is an old enemy I guess and understandably will not be trusted. But you, Romana, you want the high life deep down. It won't happen on its own around here but with an American coming into your life it could." Scott smirked.

"The high life and Americans! Scott, what are you saying? It's a bit rich. I want for nothing. Everything I want is here!" Romana retorted.

"Oh that's good, cos I don't think I can quite give you the high life. What you see is what you get," Scott replied.

"Romana, I think Scott is telling you, those are his thoughts of how we might 'play act' to get to Rodrigo."

"Oh Scott, what must you think of me?" she replied.

"I think a lot as it happens, but let's get back to the tactics of getting close to the not-so-friendly Senor Rodrigo!" Looking at me, Scott smirked again and possibly blushed at Romana's remark.

"We will play along the lines of doing some import export business with Rodrigo. I will get straight on to a guy back home and see what he can come up with. He might even have a professional interest in him. But, it will mean I will have to go back to the States to see him. I wouldn't want to try and investigate Rodrigo over the phone. Who knows, he might already have my room's phone tapped back at the hotel, or even the Ocean's Pantry for all we know!"

"When will you go?" Romana asked.

"As soon as possible, we let him know tonight that I am planning to go back to the States to sort out some business there, but will be returning shortly. Meantime, let's find out when I can fly back to make it more plausible. I'll contact my guy Gregg as soon as I get back home."

"Gregg is your contact?" I asked.

"Yeah, Gregg Stevens, he and I trained at law school, except he completed the course and decided to go into the police. I just left after a couple of years. I was kinda disenchanted, shall we say, with the whole system. It was too structured for me, too mundane. I wanted excitement in my life not just a life that meant dealing with the dregs of society. Let's just say I fell on the wrong side of the tracks. My new-found work though has taken me to many places around the world, mainly Europe going from job to job and now to here. I have to say this feels like home, so let's get this sorted and then we'll talk about the next chapter in the life of Scott Kowlowski!" Scott grinned back at me, again with that all too familiar cheeky appearance that I first saw a couple of weeks ago.

Is this finally happening, I thought? What a turn of events, it was not even two weeks ago since Scott had walked into the bar that night. Such a lot has happened in a short period of time and even more was about to happen.

"Sam will let me use his phone so we can check out the next flight back to the States. He's okay is Sam. He knows about that time. He was working at the hotel even back then. We can trust him, he won't let us down. He has his reasons too to get back at Rodrigo," I stated.

"As long as we can trust him, you will need to brief me on who is who around here, now we are talking like this. Firstly, I need to get a flight up to Miami. From there I'll travel up to New York. Gregg Stevens lives out in the suburbs on Staten

Island. I'm sure he will put me up for a couple of days which should be enough time for him to do some digging into the police records, or better still maybe even unclassified stuff. Joe, you go to Sam's now and find out what you can. Tonight we all need to understand our plan for it to work. That means in my role, I might have to say things you may not like the sound of. But please remember it's all part of the game. All three of us are just playing roles to get Rodrigo his comeuppance. Romana, all you have to do is be yourself; I will lead you, just keep with me and play along."

I had a flashing thought race through my mind at this point. Scott seemed remarkably organized in his approach to this matter. It was as if he had done this sort of thing before. No, don't be silly, I thought. I finished my coffee and left them to it on the veranda, still swinging on the hammock.

"See you back here in an hour or so." I headed out to the jeep and turned it around, in Sam's direction. Arriving there shortly afterwards, I explained our plans. Sam was all too keen to help. In three days' time there was a direct flight back to Miami from the capital just an hour or so down the coast. But, from the island of Estopona there was a flight to Miami at seven tomorrow evening. It was an airfreight flight carrying bananas – as were almost all of the flights back to the US mainland. All we had to do, would be to get Scott a three-hour ride on a trawler across to Estopona town. From there he would have to get a bus or taxi for the hour trip up to the north of the island to Puerto de Almansa. The small airport was set close on the coast near to the lush area of the island. The weather looked good, so there shouldn't be any problems crossing. Sam got straight on it and booked the flight on Scott's behalf.

"Let's go sort out the boat crossing," Sam said. I grabbed my keys for the jeep and we both headed off. Calling back in at my place we explained the situation to Romana and Scott.

"Is there any particular fisherman who might oblige?" Scott enquired.

"If you're thinking of trying to find a trustworthy one, then probably none of them. But when there are a few dollars involved, well put it this way, most would sell their own grandmother. They won't even want to know why you want a ride. Anyway, you have nothing to hide here, have you? Perhaps you could say a distant relative has just passed away and you need to get back to the States quickly. Thinking about it, that's about the size of it isn't it?" We all laughed. "C'mon, Sam, let's get going."

The quayside was busy. The fishermen had not been in very long and were just unloading their catch. The usual tourists looked on. I noticed from a distance our old friend with the poor dress sense and his garish wife, the 'Americans'. This was a chance to help the cause. Pushing nearer I shouted down to Miguel Andres.

"Miguel, Miguel!"

He looked up. "Ah Senor Joe, 'Ow are you? Okay?"

"Yes, yes I'm good. I need a favour though. Can you help me?"

"Joe, is no problem, what you want?" he said clambering up on to the quay from the deck of his boat.

Before replying I caught sight of our American friend who was staring at me. He certainly looked interested in what we were talking about. Quickly he looked away, hoping I hadn't seen him stare.

"A boat ride, not for me, but Scott. You know my young American friend? He needs to get to Estopona tomorrow. He's flying back to the States."

"When he wants to go?"

"Oh maybe two or three in the afternoon, is that okay?"

"No problem. Two is good for me; the tide will still be high. I can still go out in the morning and like today still get the best catch on the quayside to sell to the Ocean's Pantry. He will take the bus up to Puerto de Almansa? I love it up there. There is great little bar on the waterfront. I 'ave had many a good night in there, but the next morning not so good, you know!" he said, laughing out loud.

"You said you 'ave the best catch on the quay? I don't think so!" shouted a voice from over my shoulder. It was Enrico. "Hello, Joe. I am here to buy for tonight. Romana is not with you?" It was as if Enrico was in on our plan. The American had moved closer as if to listen in.

"No, I saw her earlier, but she is with Scott. I think she is giving him a tour of the town."

"Si senor, young love you think? I remember it well." He threw up his arms and shrugged his shoulders. How was it, I thought, that Enrico knew about Romana and Scott's feelings towards each other? But then again, he was a man of the world. He would have noticed the little things that would suggest such a thing. The little innuendos, the flirtatious glances Romana would make in Scott's direction when he was in her presence, just the atmosphere was somewhat different when the two of them were together.

Miguel joined in. "Heh, Enrico be careful what you say. Your beautiful wife still thinks of you as her young love!"

He laughed loudly again. "My wife is like me, so old she can't remember young love. There are some days now she can't remember my name let alone young love!" We all laughed, even the American who was now at my side.

"So Scott is heading home?" he asked.

"Oh, I didn't think you knew his name?" I queried.

"Oh, yeah," he replied hesitantly. "We spoke the other night."

He didn't sound very convincing.

"Yeah, tomorrow, back to Miami. But he'll be back again soon."

"I hear you're heading up to see Rodrigo tonight?" he stated.

"Well yeah, but how did you know, may I ask?"

"Rodrigo has invited the good lady and me up there too. It should be a real hoot!" His garish wife was now at his side grinning as only she could. This seemed a little too coincidental for my liking. This guy was not letting on all he knew and I couldn't work out who was playing whom. Rodrigo was not that clever. But this American chap, well he wasn't everything he first appeared to be, nor did I think was the wife.

There was going to be interesting times ahead for us all. The game was just beginning, and we had started without our host Senor Rodrigo. Interesting, very interesting.

"We'll see you later then around eight, I guess?" And with that he and his wife were gone.

I turned my attention back to Miguel. "I'll bring Scott down here at one thirty in good time for you to set sail then."

"Okay, no problem, sees you tomorrow."

Sam and I climbed back into the jeep.

"That American guy, he seems a bit suspicious, you know," said Sam.

"You noticed as well then. I don't know about the wife either. I reckon they are both hiding something, but what it is, is hard to contemplate just now," I shouted as I swung the jeep back towards the headland road, driving this time a lot more sedately than this morning.

"Well, perhaps you'll find out tonight," Sam answered shouting back at me.

We arrived back at my bungalow and explained the travel arrangements to Romana and Scott; we also told them what had happened with the American couple. Scott took Sam back home in my jeep. An hour or so later he was back to pick up Romana at mine. She and I had cleared up the coffee pot and cups. There was a time, and only recently, I would have left those cups for days if not weeks before washing them up. Not now though.

"See you tonight then. Rodrigo said he would have a car picking you up at seven thirty, so I'll see you a little after that," I echoed to both of them as they sped off together. I rested that afternoon and took a light snack out on to the veranda. I then snoozed till around six, rising to take a shower, dodging between the ever-temperamental hot and cold pulsation that was my meant to be my hot water.

CHAPTER SIX

I caught sight of two cars race down towards the town, one I thought must be for the American couple. The two cars soon stopped outside my bungalow and one of Rodrigo's heavies opened the rear door of the Mercedes limo. Scott and Romana sat closely together on the back seat facing forward. I sat with my back to the driver, looking backwards. Romana's long hair was loose, swept over her right shoulder. Rarely did she have her hair like this, especially when working in the Ocean's Pantry. Every now and then I caught the smell of her perfume blowing back in my direction. It was a warm, still evening. Not a cloud in the sky.

"What a beautiful evening. I wonder if there is going to be any stormy clouds on the horizon by morning though," I asked.

We all laughed quietly, enough to break the mild tension we all felt. Nothing had to be said, we could all sense it.

"Maybe, but let's not allow the evening to be spoilt by any cloudy situations," Scott replied. "I noticed the American couple had dressed for the occasion. We must look very subdued in comparison to them in our choice of dress. I think we have all chosen a more careful approach to the evening's events than they have." Scott was almost speaking in a coded manner. Romana and I got a rough idea of what he was saying and nodded.

The cars swept into the drive and came to a gentle rest outside the main door of the house. I had forgotten how splendid the house looked. Juanita had been up here for dinner once or twice, long before her fateful episode. An episode we would try this evening to start to bring to a close. She had told me how resplendent the house and gardens were. I did come up here once with her, but not for dinner. Rodrigo had asked she bring some papers from the office to the house for him to sign and I went with her. Small lights lit the drive from where we had entered, leading up to the grand main entrance steps.

Grinning, as anticipated, like a Cheshire cat Rodrigo appeared. "Welcome, welcome to you all. What a beautiful evening to be out, and Romana, you like the moon are radiant. Senora Colbert you too look, well, full of colour." Even Rodrigo had noticed the somewhat unorthodox dress sense of his dinner guest. "C'mon, let's go on to the terrace, you must see the view over the sea with moon shining on it, it is truly amazing!"

'Ma' had certainly won the 'most colourful clash you can wear' stakes, that's for sure – her violet evening dress co-ordinated perfectly with her orange wrap. Bearing in mind her shock of red hair, orange seemed to be her favourite colour. Jerry wore the white tux and cummerbund of matching orange to that of the wrap. Romana on the other hand just seemed to glide through to the terrace wearing an emerald green chiffon dress, hugging her near perfect figure. Scott and I also wore the mandatory tuxedo, but in black, and fortunately borrowed from Enrico and Sam. Needless to say mine had to have a few nips and tucks here and there.

The hall was very grand with a stairway curving up both sides of the room. We proceeded through to a drawing room study. The walls in here were adorned with large paintings. It reminded me of some old English stately home. But dare I say not as tastefully done. The view appeared and was truly fantastic. One of the servants handed us all some champagne.

"I think we all know each other, but let me do the honours anyway," Rodrigo announced. He wanted to assert his authority early in the proceedings. Pleasantries over, he then turned his attention to both Scott and our new friend Jerry.

"So where is home in the US for you then, Scott?"

"Oh, California is where I grew up, Los Angeles. But now I guess I call Miami home."

"Ever been to Texas, Scott?" chipped in Jerry.

"Just the once, I was passing through Huston on business."

"Business you say. What line of business you in?"

I noticed that Mrs Colbert, Thelma, had gone walk about. I just caught sight of her heading back into the hallway. I also decided to head that way. She was standing back from a painting, admiring it, I thought. But then to my surprise she took out from her handbag a small magnifying glass and got up close to it. Next she picked up a vase from a small round table in the corner.

"Interesting pieces don't you think? I wonder where he got them," I said, startling her.

"Er yes. You made me jump." She fumbled the glass back into her bag and removed a hanky to make it look as if that was the reason to be in the bag in the first place.

"Do you collect art, Mrs Colbert?" I enquired.

"Please call me Thelma." This was the first time the woman had spoken of her own free will as opposed to speaking through her devoted husband. "No not really. I am what you may call an enthusiastic amateur. My father has an antiques shop, so I grew up around antiques, but I have to say, none quite as splendid as these."

"Where are they from?" I quizzed.

"You have an interest in antiques as well, Mr Brampton?"

"Please, it's just Joe, but I do find these interesting."

"Okay, well Jerry has a love for this kinda of thing as well. That's how we met, in an auction house in Houston. I was there with my daddy. Joe, the way you're moochin' round out here you almost look as if you have in mind to steal them! But, somehow I don't think so!"

Her Texan drawl was slightly softer as she spoke with reason in her voice.

I smiled. "No. I am not a thief. But let's say I have an interest in these. I'd like to know where our genial host got them from."

I quickly changed the subject, having had a flash of thought. I was maybe giving too much away. Thelma smiled politely and cocked her head to one side. It was as if she had heard my thought.

"Shall we?" I said extending my hand. We returned back to the terrace where Rodrigo glanced over Scott's shoulder to see us. He made a beeline for us.

"Where are my manners, Mrs Colbert, Thelma? I have been ignoring you." Rodrigo gestured to a waiter who was holding a tray of drinks. "Please a drink, what can I get you? I have white, red, or even rosé perhaps?" Despite the fact that the ladies still had their champagne, Rodrigo was like an excited schoolboy keen to please anyone to gain attention.

"Oh rosé? Please." A popular choice for all of us except Jerry it seemed. Rarely would rosé be seen in this part of the world. Thelma commented on this fact. "I've not seen any rosé since we've been here, French too, very nice."

Rodrigo was proud to announce how he had a contact in France who sends it. "I love French wines. Come to that, I love most things French. They have such a 'chic' way about them. I do like the Italians and their style too. I don't know whether it's their clothes, their food, their wines, or more especially their art." I couldn't help but notice at this point in the conversation the fleeting glance of somewhat approval that our two American friends gave to each other at this last remark.

Rodrigo continued, "Yes they have Milan and Rome, but away from these cities, peasants almost. But even they have a kind of chic style about them. They did have one of the finest trading empires at one time during the Venetian conquests. I must say I do adore the architecture of Venice. But tonight, tonight I have taken the liberty of making the menu for dinner French. I hope you like lobster?" We all nodded approvingly. He beamed. "I hope you are all hungry?"

He linked his arm into Thelma's. "Romana, you as well, please." Like a prize peacock he strode through the large double doors of the drawing room which led out onto the terrace with the women on each arm.

"Now, I shall sit here and you two beauties will sit either side of me." The three of them sat on high backed wicker chairs which looked out across the plantation gardens and beyond. "To be surrounded by all this beauty on such a beautiful night. What more could a man wish for?"

Romana smiled an uncomfortable smile. Scott caught my eye. He too looked as though he would like to have been somewhere else at that moment.

"Wine red or white for you ladies?" Rodrigo was in full flight now. The little bull terrier in him with all its bullish ways was coming out. I saw an opportunity here and turned towards Scott. "Wine might be the answer."

Jerry held his glass of red wine up to his nose, took in the bouquet. Lowered it and for a man with such a strong Texan accent, uttered in near perfect French accent and pronunciation. "Appellation d'origine controllee! Rodrigo, you certainly do have a contact in France."

"Oh Jerry, you stop showing off now. Jerry and my daddy just love their wine. Why only last year we were in Europe to see the sights, historical ya know? Well Daddy and Jerry spent nearly every day in a cellar on a vineyard somewhere. Me, I just went shoppin' on my own as usual. But I must say them French boutiques are somethin' else. Romana honey, you would just love them!" Romana smiled nervously. She was not happy being here.

"Romana, you look troubled," said Rodrigo.

"Oh I was just thinking of the restaurant when you mentioned the menu. I hope Enrico is coping okay."

"I'm sure he is. You have left him before with no problems. Relax and let someone else do the worrying for a change," quipped Scott.

Jerry got back on the subject of France. He was eager to keep the momentum running.

"Like Thelma says, I too like my wines. I did some business, oil that is, in Marseille some years back. I, like you, fell in love with the place. The sea, the mountains and those cute little hill top villages. Sure beats the Texan landscape. Anyway, as I was sayin' it was on that trip I got into wine. I still haven't got any from the AOC though, and not through lack of tryin'!"

"AOC?" asked Scott.

"The Appellation D'Origine Controllee," Rodrigo chipped in with a voice of authority. "It is a group of vineyards in the southern region, Bellet near Nice. The rosé was a good choice. On the Riviera the locals swear it is the best rosé to have with fish. Our starter tonight is just that. Now I know, Romana, you have the best seafood restaurant for miles around. But I thought I would be cheeky and serve seafood tonight. Why? Because I bet you never sample the dishes that you offer? No, am I right?"

"Don't tell me, Bouillabaisse?" Jerry cut in using that by now almost annoying skill of his, speaking French near perfectly.

"Si, yes. I had my chef get the recipe some years ago. I love it. I hope you do too. Romana, I shall pass it on to you. Hopefully you can use it in the Ocean's Pantry? The fish are local to here and of course we have plenty of red chillies. Strangely the large tiger prawns are hard to get so I have them sent from Marseille with one of my wine consignments.

A waiter nodded to Rodrigo indicating dinner was to be served. "Shall we?" We followed Rodrigo into the dining room. The table looked splendid dressed with candles and small flower arrangements. The centrepiece was a large silver figurine.

"I see your interest in France is not restricted to the wine," Jerry commented picking up a silver fork. "Alain Saint-Joanis? The porcelain if I am not mistaken is Limoges?" Rodrigo nodded approvingly at our resident expert. I glanced across at Scott. He too nodded but in a way of question.

Surprisingly Thelma opened the conversation. "I noticed some of the pieces you have in the hallway. I thought they looked superb, but in here. Wow!"

"Oh these are nice but the really good pieces of my collection are upstairs. After dinner I will give you the guided tour. I can tell you appreciate fine things," he said pouring Thelma some more wine. Looking across the table at Jerry she cocked her head in the way I had seen out in the hallway. He smiled politely back at her. Unlike earlier when the topic of conversation was wine, Jerry seemed quite quiet just now. Questioning Rodrigo again it almost seemed Thelma had her teeth into something here and she wasn't going to let it go. Typical American I guess, straight to the point.

"You must tell me where these pieces come from. You see my daddy, he has a shop back home. He would die to see these things let alone own them like you. I bet some are real rare as well?" Rodrigo's expression became momentarily sober at this comment.

"Well yes, some are rare and I guess some would say maybe

they should be exhibited in some museum somewhere, not locked away from the eyes of millions here in my house. But art is a funny thing. I will show you a painting by Rodan, which I adore. At the time, his critics labelled it as an 'abomination of his work'! I beg to differ. Art, as we all know, is in the eyes of the beholder."

"Philippe, tell me, is farming so good here you can buy these paintings and artefacts on the back of it? I didn't think there was that much money in bananas," Scott questioned.

Again Rodrigo had his serious head on. The banana question had hit a nerve. There was a momentary silence, we all watched and waited with bated breath for his reply. It was as if our two American friends had been part of our meeting earlier that afternoon.

"Why do you ask? Is it you are thinking of becoming a farmer too?" Rodrigo quipped.

We all laughed with him. His laugh was of relief from deflecting the question quickly and cleverly. While we all laughed inside we felt almost frustration, knowing there was a hidden reason behind his huge art collection. Where had the money come from to buy this collection? Thelma, not letting go, threw in another pointed question like a thrust from a cutlass.

"So tell me, Philippe, how did you make your fortune here? You know my Jerry is in oil. I think that speaks for itself. But if he can make the same kind of numbers as you can in farming I think we need to sit down and talk, talk real serious. He's bustin' a gut doin' what he's a doin' and you seem so much more relaxed than him. I keep tellin' him to slow down or the business is a gonna kill him. But does he listen, no!"

Rodrigo threw me a glance and laughed almost nervously. "Oh I have the vines and almonds as well. They all help contribute to the profits." Jerry sat up straighter.

"Perhaps I'll buy me some land while I'm here in that case. A clean living farmer seems more appealing than oil right now."

I couldn't help myself and chipped in. "I don't know about the 'clean living' bit!" Rodrigo frowned.

"We all have our dark secrets," added Scott. "It's all part of life's rich tapestry. For instance, Joe, since you have known me you have never asked where I get my money from, have you? We are all adults here, some of us a long way from home, even you, Joe. You came here to escape to a new life, didn't you?"

For once I felt a little uncomfortable. Hopefully Scott was just playacting. I felt myself colour up around the gills.

"Well, now you put it that way, yeah. But in view of what you just said, what line of business are you in?" I said with a smile, trying to divert the attention his way.

"Import export, anything and everything. If I can find a way of moving it and make a bit then I guess you'd say I'm your man!"

"Well I just have the restaurant and that's it!" Romana cut in. There was an air of disapproval in her voice.

"Romana, I think you are the only one around this table who is an exception to this rule," Scott replied looking at everyone as he spoke.

"I don't really do anythin' much 'cept shop. But I think some of my Jerry's 'Huggy Bears' dealings are done away from prying eyes and ears," quipped Thelma winking at Jerry as she did.

Jerry backed her up in their philosophy of how they justified their actions. "I reckon if it don't hurt no-one then that's okay. I might have done the odd dodgy deal. But it ain't never meant someone getting hurt in any shape or way. That's just not my style. Anyway, it keeps a whole economy running, don't it? It might be a bit on the grey-come-black side of the market. Well, I'll tell ya, I'll buy and sell anythin'. Hell, I've done the lot. If there's been a dollar to be had I've been there at the front of the queue. Ya see oil's what I know. But I also know the people who want to deal in oil too. Now they are greedy, especially down Africa way. You get the odd up and coming dictator who thinks he'll be a millionaire over night. They know they have to sell at what would be low prices on the legit market. But, to be legit would mean the intervention of the authorities within the industry, and they don't want that, do they? If you get what I mean."

The rest of dinner was fairly uneventful with the usual small talk about the area and some of the characters that lived around here. Although Rodrigo was getting decidedly louder as his wine glass was continually being filled by Scott who was sat opposite him. He did remark at one point he appeared to be the only one drinking. Scott interjected by saying he, like most of us, was only drinking the white, when really it was the table water. Rodrigo being the only one except me on the red. Needless to say my drinking habits of old meant that I was still perfectly sober. Well certainly in comparison to him.

Dinner over, Jerry asked for that tour of the house. It was almost said in a hurried eager tone of voice. Romana was relieved to get up from the table. She got up and walked directly to Scott's side linking her arm in his. "Keep smiling," he whispered to her.

We went back into the hallway and up the impressive staircase. "So, who are these people? Not your ancestors I know," said Jerry.

"No, not my ancestors, but like me they would have been land owners and wealthy merchants."

"Where have they come from? I mean where do you buy such fine pieces of art?" Rodrigo turned at that point as if Jerry had hit that nerve again, was he becoming suspicious of him?

"Oh, you would be surprised where you can buy such pieces."

There was an element of anger in his voice. But this was quickly followed by that wry smirk of his. Jerry and Thelma nodded to each other taking particular notice of a portrait of a man dressed in a costume of silver sleeves and tunic. The trousers were bright orange. Standing there he looked directly at the observer. In his hand was a sort of baton; the other was out-stretched above a helmet from a suit of armour. A young lad was holding this. The darkened sky behind him helped to illuminate his costume. He certainly was a proud man, albeit a young one – perhaps only twenty or thirty.

"You like that one as well?" Scott interjected.

"Yes I do, it's a Dobson, William Dobson 1642 or 3, an English painter. He was commissioned by the royal household to follow the up and coming Charles II. Document his life I guess you would say. No cameras back then, just these fine beautiful paintings from that time in history. It shows the young Charles or Prince of Wales as he is there, in his entire splendour." Jerry had given his explanation with an irreverent passion to which we were all left virtually speechless. Again, our American friends were proving to be something different and deeper than we first thought. Quite a double act, I thought.

"Wow, you certainly know your stuff," Scott exclaimed almost loudly, thankfully breaking the rather frigid atmosphere.

We moved along like a party of tourists following Rodrigo who was too caught up in showing off his fine collection to notice yet again the pointed questions aimed at him. It may have been the drink or just his naive grasp on the situation.

Moving along the upper hallway, small and large tables almost creaked from the weight of huge vases or statues, more pictures adorned the walls.

As we toured the hallway I caught sight of Jerry and Thelma. They were both standing quite motionless looking up at a picture, a landscape. I moved towards them.

"I spend every day in this landscape, with its beautiful slopes. Indeed, I cannot imagine a more pleasant way or place to pass my time," Jerry muttered.

"That's rather poignant if I may say so, Jerry."

"You may, Joe. There are not my words, far from it. Cezanne, 1906! He wrote it in a letter to his son. This painting went missing twenty-nine years ago whilst being moved from the Lourve in Paris back to Aix-en-Provence for 'safe keeping' from damage – as of course Paris was suffering by way of Allied bombing. His studio was there, still is, and left just as he left it. There are unfinished canvases, palettes and his old black hat. He was from the region and painted many landscapes. But it was nearly always of this Mont-ste-Victoire. That one," he said, pointing to another picture which was housed in a very heavily carved wooden frame, "is a van Gogh. It's called Café de Nuit painted by him in the late 1880s while he lived in Arles, a small town west of Marseille. This one disappeared some twenty or thirty years ago from the private collection of a French dignotaire. Two security guards were shot in the robbery. Rodrigo I would say certainly has blood on his hands. If not his, indirectly he is involved. So now we have to find his French contact, if indeed they are French."

Thelma turned to me. "I think by now you know we are not your average American tourists. It would insult your intelligence to say otherwise, wouldn't it?" She said this quite matter-of-factly with a slightly softer accent, losing her harsher Southern drawl.

"Yes, now you say that. Even with the wine the old grey cells have been working overtime just now. I appreciate your comment but that said, here and now is not the best place to discuss it, don't you think?" I replied quietly for fear of Rodrigo listening in on us. She politely nodded.

"Okay, that's the paint. That just leaves the powder!" Thelma said turning to Jerry, again losing her strong Texan accent.

Finally at the end of the hall a pair of doors, so heavily carved they looked like they should have stood at the entrance to a church, were thrown open with gusto by Rodrigo. This seemed to be the piece de la resistance.

We all gasped in awe as Rodrigo grinned like a Cheshire cat. "This is art!" he exclaimed. "With, I think you will agree, a capital A!" Now laughing aloud, Rodrigo strode into the vast room with his arms outstretched, spinning like a small child.

"Come! We must dance!" He clapped his hands twice and at the far end of the room other doors opened to a small stage with a quartet. Bemused, we all looked at each other. Rodrigo spun around and made a beeline for Romana.

"Tonight we will enjoy!"

Scott on the other hand sensed Romana's mood of discontent and excused Rodrigo saying how he had promised Romana that at the first sound of music he would dance with her, what with leaving for the States tomorrow this might be his last chance for a while. Rodrigo gestured his approval but muttered they would dance before the night was over.

Scott used the time dancing to remind Romana of our mission. He pulled her close to him and appeared to be whispering sweet nothings to her. "I know we can't talk too much just now, but our two new friends, and I think I'm right when I say friends, I reckon they know more than meets the eye. From what Joe was telling me while you were out on the terrace, Jerry has more than a passing interest in art than he is making out."

I was mindful of Rodrigo's narrowing eyes as he looked towards the young couple. He might have had a skinful of red wine, but he also appeared to be almost straining to listen to what Scott was saying to Romana.

"Philippe, how about you have another drink?" I asked. Knowing he wouldn't refuse, he scampered off to organize some more refreshments. This gave me the opportunity to cut in on Jerry and Thelma.

"I don't want to sound rude, Joe, but do you mind if I sit this one out? Dancing ain't really my thing, I felt obliged with Senor Rodrigo and all, you know?" Thelma apologized.

"Thank heavens for that. I just fancied a chat about some of these paintings," I answered, smiling at her. Jerry also took the opportunity to sit. It was warm in the room but two minutes of exercise for Jerry, who wasn't quite the 'racing snake' physique of his youth, welcomed the rest.

Jerry looked to be concentrating intensely. He pushed his bottom lip out and narrowed his eyes. Looking across at Scott and Romana he shook his head having come to a conclusion of his own. Standing up he drew me into his confidence by talking in a lower tone.

"Joe, it seems to me that you guys know something ain't quite right round here. Thelma, before you say anything, I know I should have consulted with you first. But hell it's smacking us all across the face ain't it?" Thelma smiled.

"Well I guess you can say you beat me to it." I looked across at the two lovebirds that were lost for the moment still smooching on the dance floor. Jerry continued, "We all need to meet to discuss this further. Thelma and me, we're working undercover for the FBI but also in collaboration with Interpol in Europe. We specialise in fine art and antiquities for the FBI back in the US. We have been trying to pin down Rodrigo for what seems forever. But, whenever we get close to connecting him, the scent goes stale and we have always drawn a blank. There have been a series of art thefts across Europe for some years now; in fact a lot went missing during the last war. We know Hitler virtually raped Europe of art even before 1939. A lot of Jewish art dealers lost an awful lot of pieces and then the majority of them paid with their lives in the camps. Over that time it was always suspected the various works went out of Europe to South America. Not only that, a lot of Nazis made their way down into South America after the war as well. There were 'rat runs' from Europe into Brazil, Chile, Paraguay, Uruguay and more. As many as five thousand went to Argentina. The ironic thing here is that Rodrigo's love of everything Italian kinda fits in with this. You see we know the Vatican and the Italian government of the time assisted Nazi officers who had held high positions within the Third Reich's ranks to escape down this way. As you know, South America is a huge continent and we think Rodrigo can lead us to not all, but maybe some of these guys. If he does, well then that will mean lying to rest a lot of people's heartache and anguish from that dark time. All known suspects to the authorities across Europe have been accounted for. That is the majority of Hitler's inner core group. Some were murdered some had taken their own lives. But a huge number have just plain disappeared off the face of the earth. Until now that is. Now is neither the time nor the place. All I will say is some of these paintings should be hung up elsewhere on other walls, if you get my drift?"

"Yes I get it, let's say we meet at the Ocean's Pantry when Scott gets back, okay?"

Rodrigo appeared again still full of joy with himself, or was it red wine? Oblivious to our brief conversation he brought in some more wine.

"I'd love some coffee if I may?" Thelma asked.

"Of course I will send for some straightaway." In his

absence I quickly told Scott and Romana of my chat with Jerry.

"Why the trip back home then, Scott?" Jerry enquired.

"Well in view of what has been said, I am going back to make a few inquiries of my own with an old friend based in the New York police department. I don't know he might turn up something on Rodrigo and his past. He seems to have made it pretty big over here, especially seeing that the main crop is bananas."

"Oh, you're right. He has made it big. But I don't know if your friend will find anything. You see Rodrigo is the subject of a much bigger inquiry. There's a lot going on here that you might be real surprised to hear."

"We must look a little suspicious all huddled together chatting away as we are." We all spun round to see Rodrigo enter the room again with a waiter carrying a tray of coffee. Luckily Jerry was facing the entrance and acted instinctively.

"Truth is, we are discussing your remarkable collection. I love the Cezanne in the hall out there."

Rodrigo smiled politely whilst gesturing the waiter to put the tray on a table near to us. "The landscape, ah yes I too love to get lost in its frame as he did," he said in an almost knowingly fashion.

Coffee was had by all and the conversation continued with small talk about the estate and the area. Rodrigo was a little cagey about what was grown on the estate when asked innocently by Scott. I noticed Jerry throw a sideward glance towards Thelma. Again with an almost knowingly expression of interpretation before Rodrigo answered. "Oh, um, just bananas, coconuts for export. Then, um, the regular crops of vegetables which we sell to the markets across the region here."

Scott drew attention to the time and his trip back to the States the next day. "I'll be back in three or four days and if it is not too presumptuous of me I would love to have a tour of your estate?"

"But of course, how inattentive of me. Yes you must, all of you, if you wish that is?" Rodrigo replied eagerly. "Right then that's sorted I will escort you back downstairs to your cars." The time had come in the evening when the conversation was running thin and subconsciously we all wanted to be on our way sooner rather than later. Nodding to Jerry and Thelma as if to reiterate our pending rendezvous we left the driveway and headed back down towards the beach road.

"You drop me first if that's okay. I guess you two will want a night cap?" Romana turned round to me and smirked.

"Yes, Uncle, we will drop you off first."

CHAPTER SEVEN

I called in at the restaurant early afternoon asking Romana if she had heard from Scott.

"No, he said he would call hopefully tonight from Miami."

We didn't talk much if at all. I repaired a leaking tap in the kitchen and cleaned out a sink waste that was slow in draining away in the laundry room. Romana as usual busied herself in and around the kitchen preparing for the evening meals. A couple of the fishermen dropped by for a drink after their haul had been sorted and sold.

Sitting with Enrico I enjoyed a light snack that would see me through till breakfast next day. Scott phoned and spoke to Romana just to say it had been an uneventful trip and he was now at a small motel just off the airport in Miami. He had called Gregg Stevens and was flying up to New York on the eight thirty morning flight. He would call her again from there when he was settled in at Gregg's.

Much the same happened the following day except that I put in a full day's work in order to keep my mind from wandering, or is that wondering about Scott's return? Would he come back with enough information to nail Rodrigo once and for all? Based on what Jerry had said I didn't think so but the thought kept my spirits high. One way or another I felt certain that Rodrigo's days of living it up at the expense of others were numbered.

On day three of Scott's absence I spent it cleaning up a bit around the bungalow. Taking my second espresso of the morning on to the balcony I watched the lads catching the growing surf. It was always the way. By ten the surf would start to gather as the off-shore breezes did so as well. I guess you could say that nothing got going too early in these parts. Scott had called Romana as promised a couple of nights ago with no news other than to say he had arrived safely and had contacted his old police acquaintance and arranged to meet the next day. He wouldn't call again but would tell us all on his return. That return was in fact today. He would sail back into the harbour with Miguel on the evening tide.

I had caught sight of Jerry and Thelma in the afternoon, but not to talk to. They walked along the beach just after one, right past the bungalow. I think they knew where I lived. It was as if they had been keeping a low profile. Maybe I was being just a bit suspicious of anything and everyone. Who knows?

Finally, at around seven I left home for the Ocean's Pantry. Not wishing to appear too anxious I parked my jeep up at the side of the kitchen entrance. The anticipation I felt was greater than that of a child on Christmas morning.

Scott greeted me, shaking my hand and smiling broadly as only he could. Carrying a beer and glass, Romana appeared.

"I heard the screech of brakes. I said to Scott that was you. I thought you might have been here earlier to greet him?" I took the glass and bottle from her.

"No, I thought you two might like at least five minutes to yourselves before the old fool turned up."

"Uncle Joe, two things, you are not an old fool," remarked Romana.

"And the second thing is?" I asked.

"Pour your beer into the glass and don't drink it from the bottle!" She laughed giving me a hug.

We sat down at what I affectionately called 'Romana's table'. Of course as Scott pointed out, they were all in fact 'Romana's tables'. Again we laughed as we sat in the corner overlooking the harbour view we all liked the most.

"Well? Come on, the suspense is killing me. What did you find out about Rodrigo?"

"Nothing of any detail anyway. It was just as Jerry had said. It would appear that there is a big operation going on trying to connect Rodrigo with the art thefts across Europe. Gregg Stevens, my old college friend, did some digging before I arrived. All information using Rodrigo's name drew a blank. All files were sanctioned as 'authorized access only'. Unfortunately Gregg is not authorized to get that info the only way to access those files is through the FBI or Interpol it would seem." Jerry and Thelma had said the same.

"Our friend or not, as the case may be, Senor Rodrigo is some big fish in the world of art theft, and there is an awful lot of people trying to hook him out of the water and wring him out to dry! What I can tell you is that he is also linked to other things. Exports, shall we say, from Europe to here is one thing. But it's the exports from here to the US that throws a completely different angle on to the situation. He's been running drugs to the States for years."

"I knew it!" I said banging my fist on the table. "Oh sorry, ever since that night I knew it, and now I know it for certain."

"Miguel told me on the trip over how many years ago some of the fishermen on the quayside had been approached by Rodrigo's men to run drugs to the States. Especially, when the fishing hauls were thin on the ground if you know what I mean?"

"Have you eaten yet, Uncle Joe?" Romana asked.

"No, I haven't had much all day to be honest. Not too hungry really, I guess it's been in anticipation of Scott's findings."

"Well talking of food, we are starving, how about your finest table for five please, mine host!" Jerry bellowed as he and Thelma came into the restaurant from the quayside.

"You couldn't hear what we were saying could you?" I asked.

"Only the bit about the food, you know us Yanks – we love our food! How'd you get on, Scott? Find out much?"

Scott explained again to Jerry and Thelma what he had told us.

"The FBI eh?" Jerry said in a questioning tone. Thelma opened her unusually large handbag taking out some papers. She also put a couple of badges on the table. Both her and Jerry's picture was recognizable to me. Not having my glasses on, I couldn't read the writing.

"My god, you two are both in the FBI!" Romana whispered.

"For our sins I guess, yes," Thelma said.

"Look, as we said a couple of nights ago, you all know something is not on the level with Rodrigo. We've been trying to pin something on him for years. Not Jerry and me, but the Bureau has. This isn't just about the art though. We are sure he might lead us either directly or indirectly to some pretty unpleasant people who made their way down here during the forties and fifties. Scott, we knew you would draw a blank in New York. But it can maybe get us closer to Rodrigo, the fact that you went. Jerry will explain."

"He thinks that following our dinner the other night that you are up for a bit of import, export. Well I think we exploit his greed by setting up a deal to import something that is dear to his heart. A painting! The drugs he runs, our vice guys are ready to pounce. They now have enough witnesses along the chain of supply to lock him up for ever."

"So why not move now? Why wait to pin a stolen painting on him?" Scott interjected.

"It's politics, Scott, pure and simple politics. Who owns priceless art? Who can afford it? It doesn't matter if they are wealthy public figures, or eccentric business tycoons. There are a number of these people who in turn know people. They have been taken for a ride in their eyes by some small time crook in South America. They are, in their opinion, big league; Rodrigo on the other hand is just 'small town village green'. Sure, in these parts a big fish in a small tank. But in their world he's just plankton! You could say the net is being drawn in now."

"Okay, so where do I fit in on this?" Scott asked.

"Joe, you know when you spoke to me the other night when we were in the hall? I was looking at a picture. A picture which at today's value in an auction house would be somewhere in the region of 10 million dollars! That painting was stolen eighteen years ago from a private collection belonging to an oil tycoon in Texas. He never got the insurance back on it because he never got it insured. He was assured by the security company he employed to fit his security system that his home was impossible to penetrate. He's like some of my fellow Texans, voiced a little too loudly that fact. A month after he bought it in Paris it was stolen from him. He lost all face with some of his business partners and he suffered doing any business deals within the oil industry as well. He was fondly remembered for having barbed wire around his house made from string. You see as I said before, people know people. He didn't just lose a painting. He lost a whole business empire by having that painting stolen. He, like a good few others, wants Rodrigo put away and made an example of. The art world is fickle with reclusive people who move in their own small niche circle of connections. He does not fit in with those circles."

"And what about that painting, you were going to say?" I asked.

"That painting, what do you remember of it, Joe?" Thelma asked.

"I remember you had a magnifying glass looking at it?"

"Yes I did. I didn't know that you had seen me though. I must be more careful in future," she said with a smile.

"Umm, if my memory serves me well it was a canal in Venice."

"Yes, you're right. It was a scene of a canal in Venice. The canal to be exact is the 'Grand Canal' in Venice. The entrance to the city from the lagoon and it was painted by Turner during his Grand Tour of Europe. He did a whole bunch of them, eight in all."

'There was a whole bunch of them'– I couldn't help thinking how both Thelma and Jerry, although highly knowledgeable about the art world, sometimes lacked a basic command of the English language.

She continued, "He travelled through Europe going into Switzerland, Germany, Italy and finishing in France. While there in Paris, in rented rooms, he accurately painted what he had sketched on his travels. It was always commented on at the time by his fellow travellers how he had a sketch pad with him at all times. He once offered to pay for his train ticket by sketching the portrait of the conductor. The conductor was not having any of it and Turner had to offer one of his fellow passengers the same gesture. In turn they paid for his onward travel.

"Did you also notice to the right of that Venice scene a framed letter? Hand-written I must say and not completely, clear or visible to the naked eye. It's certainly taken a bit of a bashing over the years. It starts something like, 'have seen Turner several times – and have been in that wonderful old house – where the old woman with her head wrapped up in dirty flannel used to open the door and where on faded walls hardly weather-tight – and among bits of old furniture thick with dust like a place that has been forsaken for years, were those brilliant pictures all glowing with sunshine and colour'.

"It was written by one Lady Trevelyan. She wrote it to a Dr John Brown in October 1852. They were both admirers of Turner's work having done the Grand Tour themselves. Remember, there were no Kodak's back then to take your snap shots with."

Her explanation sounded not unlike a history teacher in front of a class as she continued to add more detail.

"Anyway, the Bridge of Sighs and six other Venetian scenes completed by him at the same time were stolen from various collections in the States and one from England. The Bridge of Sighs was from our man in Texas. At one time they were all displayed in the Tate in London along with the letter and some other artefacts of Turner's. It was only then did anyone see these works together. That was some twenty years ago. The letter was owned by a wealthy businessman in London along with two of the Venetian scenes – one being Entrance to Grand Canal, and the other, Venice: The Piazzetta and the Doge's Palace from the Bacino. These were reputed to be the finest of the eight in this collection of what Turner painted on this trip. Two months after the Tate showing, Entrance to Grand Canal was stolen along with the letter. The other works, with the exception of one, were stolen from various other collections over the next three years from that time. However, one is still on display at the Tate in London – The Doge's Palace. Now, it would appear possible that as Rodrigo has got the letter and the Grand Canal painting. He could well have the other London paintings, could he not?"

"What do you mean? Rodrigo could have one of the two paintings? We saw the Entrance to Grand Canal on his wall didn't we?" I asked.

"Yes, but we have to verify its authenticity. That's why I had the magnifying glass on it," Thelma explained. "We need to get back into that house to see all of what Rodrigo has on show. Check it is the genuine article. He has stuff hidden away, I just know it. Remember at dinner how he commented on the 'Italian peasants' with the exception of Venice? We are getting so close now to getting him. You guys have helped us get the break none of us have been able to get for years."

"How's that?" Scott asked.

Jerry explained how the Tate in London was to have an exhibition in a matter of weeks. Works from all over Europe were to be shown there. Both sculpture and paintings, all of which had not seen the light of day let alone a museum for possibly years. It had been widely published within the art world.

"I gotta tell you, as much as I love art of pretty much all forms. This runs deep with me. It ain't just about the art now. It was just over ten years ago we found out about the ex-Nazi officers escaping here. Now the art that the Nazis plundered across all Europe from the early to mid-thirties are pretty much common knowledge. I'm not condoning the thefts from the galleries of Europe, but you could say that against the horrific crimes to the people of Europe by the Nazis, these thefts kinda pale into insignificance. But, they did, as we know, some pretty gruesome stuff back then and they need to be brought to justice. Then there is the 'now'. This art is being bought with dirty money gained through unscrupulous methods, selling drugs that are ruining our kids today and in the future. It's killing these kids, taking away from them any kind of life experiences they might have and enjoy without taking this crap. The way I see it, Rodrigo has burned the candle along with a lot of nasty people at both ends now for far too long."

Thelma went on to tell us about suspected Nazi war criminals that they had been able to capture. There was Adolf Eichmann who under his alias of Ricardo Klement got to Argentina in '52 with his family and worked seemingly innocently at a car plant. He did this for some ten years until he was traced by the Bureau in 1961. No-one had suspected him as someone who had, less than twenty years previous, been the right hand man to the SS Chief, Heinrich Himmler in the Third Reich, who was responsible for the trains that carried millions to their deaths at the extermination camps in Nazi-occupied Poland. Under the war crimes treaty Eichmann was sent to Israel in '62 where he was hanged for his crimes to the Jewish people. But it would seem there are still many, many more to be traced. We know of an organization called ODESSA which was formed by former SS members.

I would even go so far as to say Rodrigo is German. Apart from the odd sentence here and there, we have not heard him speak fluent Spanish. He won't be the first or indeed the last."

Thelma went on to inform us even more about what had happened since the war. It was hard for me to comprehend that those who I had fought against in Europe, the very people who had committed hideous crimes on the innocent people had like me, fled to South America. Albeit, for far different reasons.

"They were called 'ratlines' from Europe passing through Italy, France and other European countries all with the same destiny, South America. We have found out that there were two networks operating. One was through the CIA and the other through believe it or not, the Vatican, known at the time as OSS – the Overseas Secret Service. It had a whole flight network set up connecting many European cities, meaning there was never a direct route. So several flight paths were available, reducing the suspicion of where these monsters were going. Over the years we have been able to track down around two and a half thousand Nazi leaders who ended up on this vast continent. The Vatican route, called 'the route of the monasteries' or 'the path of the rats', was the most effective. Who would suspect this mighty religious body to be party to such a thing? Nearly all of these escapes were planned by the conspirators of the Maison Rouge in Strasbourg. Its headquarters were in the Vatican City, operating from offices under the umbrella of the Pontifical Commission of Assistance. Because of the support given by the Vatican and the Italian people many fugitives who had committed war crimes were able to escape. By the end of 1946 Peron opened his arms to these criminals, welcoming them into Argentina. The church known as the Argentinean Delegation of Immigration in Europe, whose headquarters were located in Rome, had made Peron a man of their church. General Peron's close friend, Jose Silva, was the church's priest. He immediately went to Italy with instructions to organise the junction of four million Europeans into Argentina. That meant some thirty thousand people a month would be entering the country. The Dictorate of Migration in Buenos Airies organised everything needed to get the immigrants from Europe into Argentina as quickly as possible. There was entry permits, Red Cross passports and visas needed to be issued by the Argentinian consulate. We only realised this huge movement was happening simply because of a tip-off from someone who was working at the dockside in Genoa. One night in a port-side bar, he had said how there was an increase in ships going between Genoa and Buenos Airies, all of which were only ever the Dodero Line. It also unravelled the ODESSA organization as well. This was made up of and run by ex-SS members. Now this network was a secret collaboration of Nazi groups to help the escape of SS members from Germany into Spain and South America. As many stayed in Madrid as the number who left for Brazil, Argentina or other parts of South America. But one by one we are finding them and bringing them to justice."

Jerry brought the conversation back to here and now. He was confident Scott was the man to get close to Rodrigo. He felt Rodrigo had a certain sort of empathy towards Scott. He could see in Scott a similar character to maybe how he saw himself at that age. Scott was to start getting close to Rodrigo. When he had gained his confidence, he would tell Rodrigo of the planned theft. Scott's involvement in the theft would be through an old acquaintance from college, Paul Radeon Junior. He was the son of a known safe blower suspected for acquiring several works of art to order from across Europe.

The Tate was to bring together one of the grandest collections of art including sculptures as well as paintings. As far as Rodrigo was concerned, Scott would be arranging all the logistics regarding the transport, following and monitoring all the pieces which were to be picked up from various locations across Europe. It would seem that Scott's brief time in the police would finally bear fruit and come into play. His two or three years in the force had been spent working undercover. As a young impressionable man he got just that bit too close to living this fake way of life. Ultimately it led him astray. All the works would come together at a location just south of Paris. Once there, they would be brought together and securely loaded into one container truck. This would then be driven to the coast at Le Havre to cross to the English Channel docking at Dover.

It would be a small team of just four. The FBI had already planted a man some months before who had now built up relationships with the Tate and was fully involved in the transportation across Europe for them. Bear in mind of course, the Tate was not aware of the forthcoming theft.

The plan was to make the hit on the crossing. The security at this point would be at its slackest based on having the insider travelling the whole journey he would be able to co-ordinate and order the security guards accordingly. No-one would be allowed on the cargo deck when it sailed and all doors to the cargo deck would be sealed for the crossing. Scott and the other two FBI guys would remain in another truck on the same cargo deck and as close to their target as possible. Once the ferry was in the open sea beyond Le Havre's harbour they would get to work.

This second truck would have an identical load. As the original paintings were loaded along the way the inside guy would be giving instructions as to where and how they should be secured in the truck. Scott and his team meanwhile would be noting exactly where they had to re-position their load of fakes when swopping the cases from truck to truck. All the packaging would be identical in its marking and colour. So when docked in Dover the returning drivers would, under instruction from our FBI insider, check the load to see that all was well. They would continue to London for the final part of their journey none the wiser. Only when arriving and un-loading would the heist come to light. By this time our shipment would be down on the south coast at Southampton being loaded on to a ship bound for South America.

"But why not just ship the fakes down here for Rodrigo without having to go to all this trouble?" I asked.

"Rodrigo will be watching, albeit from a distance. But he has his contacts and we need to make sure the robbery is slapped all across the papers, worldwide. This will fuel his ego, knowing he stands a good chance of getting these pieces and by taking them from under the noses of some of the biggest collectors in Europe. Can you imagine Rodrigo if that happens? He won't be able to contain himself round here. Also, Rodrigo does know his stuff. He will check the pieces out with a fine toothed comb to see he is getting the genuine article," Thelma explained.

Jerry and Thelma would brief Scott on what he would be telling Rodrigo and what was to happen. This would be that once the paintings were at the Tate, it would be broken into with by a discreet small team being involved. They didn't trust Rodrigo one bit. Jerry thought his loose tongue might blow the cover on the operation if he was told by Scott how the switch was too really going to happen. If Rodrigo were to show off or let his tongue slip to any of his contacts in the underworld the whole operation would be blown. The FBI wanted him to do the deal, albeit with them, they needed to catch him red handed with the paintings in his procession and have him use the drugs as payment.

After a lot of run-throughs with Jerry and Thelma to get his story straight, Scott knew what he would be telling Rodrigo. There would be an inside guy who would get them into the Tate, but not into the main viewing gallery where the paintings were displayed. This was because at least four people have keys and security codes to each of the different gallery rooms. Obviously the codes change daily, sometimes a few times during the course of the day. To get all four of any of these key holders to work like this on the inside is virtually impossible, but Scott and his team had been working for months to gain the trust of four such guards. They would need a cut, but in the bigger scheme of things, it was next to nothing compared to what Scott and Rodrigo were to gain. Plus, an explosives guy would be needed to gain entry into the main display gallery. Once inside, the safe man would be needed to disarm the combination number sequences on the security door systems that the Tate has for all their exhibits. Again, these codes will change on a daily basis.

Now, although this is to be an inside job, they want to make it known that there will be somethin' goin' down. It will also have to appear to be authentic. So they will make a few murmuring sounds to the underworld that there is a job about to happen. Quite simply, the 'safe man' will get a bit drunk in a favourite watering hole where known criminals hang out. If word got out about the possible job, as sure as eggs are eggs, after the event these guys will more than likely spill the beans in order to protect their owns skins.

Scott had a lot of studying to do in order to brush up on his art knowledge, names of known thieves who specialize in art and artefacts. There were also the names and backgrounds of people who collect sought after works, straight or otherwise. All of this would help him gain the confidence of Rodrigo. Part of all this research and homework would include finding out exactly what Rodrigo specifically loved when it came to art. Scott would say how he had contacts in the art world, but didn't necessarily know a great deal about the artworks he had acquired to order. This would fuel Rodrigo's ego. But what Scott was really interested in was making money, lots of money.

Jerry and Thelma continued to brief him on how the Tate would be oblivious to the heist. To the world it would appear a robbery had taken place. The genuine paintings were still to be used to hand over to Rodrigo, or at least whoever would be doing the deal on his behalf. But Jerry and Thelma were pretty confident Rodrigo would be present when the shipment was to be traded. Collectors who had had works stolen were obviously keen to get justice served against whoever had carried out the crimes. If they got back their priceless works, well that would be even better. Suffice to say, most had written off the loss. If Rodrigo had so much as a sniff of a fake it would jeopardize the whole aim of getting him locked up. Besides, it wasn't just the paintings that held the value here; it would be stopping all the drugs that Rodrigo could otherwise peddle to the kids on the streets across Europe. Rodrigo was understood to be one of the biggest drug barons in the South American continent.

Scott was to arrange a surprise 'return from America' dinner at the Ocean's Pantry for Rodrigo. Scott would just dine with Philippe and Romana. Both Scott and Romana would be carrying a concealed microphone. Meanwhile, Jerry and Thelma would be listening in on everything being said and record it on to a tape machine rigged up in an upstairs room of the restaurant. This recording could then be used later as supporting evidence, if of course everything went to plan. Rodrigo had to take the bait first for anything to progress. Even the topic of conversation was almost scripted by Jerry and Thelma.

It was crucial at this first meeting that Scott was able to get the ball rolling and engage Rodrigo in at least having some remote interest in being involved in a theft that would result in him getting some pieces of priceless pieces of art to add to his already huge collection. Ideally they would get into the detail of how such a heist could work for them. At the least, Rodrigo would want to go away and give it some thought.

Scott questioned Thelma. "What if he just doesn't want to play ball? What am I to do?"

Thelma smirked. "Not a chance. Believe me; he won't be able to resist such an opportunity. He's like one of those junkies with a bad habit, he feeds with the crap he ships. He's addicted. No, don't worry, he'll want to play ball!"

The whole meal had been planned by Jerry and Thelma like a military operation in all its detail. They briefed Romana and Scott on not just the subject of conversation but also the timings of what was an important event. They would start with polite chit chat. Then the weather of the last few days and what was it like here whilst Scott had been away. What was the drive from the estate down to the restaurant this evening? The conversation would then focus on the area as a whole and how business had come and gone around these parts. Jerry was keen for Scott to make continuous albeit subtle hints how he wanted to get involved in some kind of business or certainly at least make money, and plenty of it for him and Romana. The meat platter starter with olives and dips would be enough time to exhaust the niceties of day to day life.

Once the main course fish dish was on the table, this was the cue to step up the conversation to a more realistic and relevant subject – a subject that was never far from Philippe Rodrigo's mind – the subject of making money. Hopefully Rodrigo would get an underlying feeling that Scott was keen to make big sums of cash and may be even prepared to take some big risks to achieve his goal. By the time dessert was due to be served the seed would have been planted. Romana would politely excuse herself around this time, saying she was going to check on the kitchen, and anyway dessert was not for her. During the course of the meal Scott would have plied enough wine down Rodrigo's neck to gain his confidence and tell him how he had plans to pull off a major job that would rock both the authorities and the art world as a whole. The key here was that whatever wine Rodrigo drank, Scott would have maybe a couple of glasses, but opt for a different wine that was on the table. Needless to say this was to be no more than a grape juice. Scott had to remain focused at all times. One false fact or statement from Scott if quizzed by Rodrigo could blow the whole operation out of the water. So much was at stake here to ultimately get Rodrigo behind bars and close down his drug running to both Europe and the United States.

He would also say how one of his contacts was keen for him to get involved in a job in London. If Rodrigo took the bait, and Jerry was sure he would, Scott would leave shortly after this dinner meeting. The major job was scheduled to happen in six to eight weeks' time. On completion Scott would travel south-east from London to Singapore for a few days before moving on to Australia, staying a week there before coming back to our neck of the woods via the States.

The painting would meantime be in a container from Southampton, England along with a load of weaving machine spares from a factory in Leeds. The team unloading at this end would be hand-picked to sort the container's cargo accordingly. Scott would pick up the crate which the paintings would be in and bring it back here to Rodrigo's house. He would be alone at all times, only being watched from afar by the FBI. Thelma pointed out again that if Rodrigo grew at all suspicious she was sure that Rodrigo would have no hesitation in having Scott removed from the scene.

The only person around the table not smiling at the thought of the heist was of course Romana. She remained quiet throughout the whole of the briefing. I watched as she got up and walked to the kitchen. Glancing back her expression said a thousand words. I got up, mumbling 'excuse me'.

Romana spoke quietly, "I don't want him to risk his life for a few old paintings, Uncle Joe."

"I know, but I think even you would agree there is a side to Philippe Rodrigo you were not aware of until now? Forget the paintings, what about the drugs? You heard Jerry say the FBI drugs boys are going to deal with that. Scott won't be too involved. Just think, those drugs end up killing kids on the streets of cities. Kids just like you and Scott. Just think how that will help end the misery of youngsters like you two. He will be safe, you heard them say the FBI won't move in on Rodrigo till the painting is hanging on his wall. Scott may not even be there at the house at that time when they go running in."

"Yes I realise that but what about when the money is handed over? What if Rodrigo doesn't stand by his word and pay Scott what's agreed? What if one of his guards steps in? It could get so dangerous for him."

"I know, so I will be wearing a bullet-proof vest and carrying a bit of protection myself," Scott interjected, standing in the doorway of the kitchen.

"We've got to do this, Romana. I want to do this. This man is not nice, to say the least. The paintings, well I agree with you, they are just paintings some old guy did way back when. They now hang in a museum no-one goes to or in a house where definitely no-one sees them. Romana, remember this is the same man that killed your mother. We can't prove that and bring him to justice – we only know what Joe and old Sam have told us. Based on what I have heard and now know, this needs to be done. I have every trust in Jerry and Thelma along with their FBI colleagues. I need to do this, Romana. If for nothing else, I need to do it for you."

"I hope you mean that and are not doing it for some reward?"

"The only reward for me in all of this is for me to stay here with you and help run the Ocean's Pantry," he said, grinning.

"If you think you are going to help in my restaurant you can think again! Enrico and I run the kitchen and Uncle Joe deals with the maintenance!" Her fiery Latin temper exploded. I tried to extinguish the heat of her wrath but before I could she ran to Scott putting her arms around his neck.

"You must be careful. I understand and you are right, he needs to be punished. In any case, Uncle Joe will retire soon; so you could be useful doing the maintenance!"

We all laughed, Romana linking her arms into ours and we rejoined Thelma and Jerry.

"We all set then? Do I make the call to get things rolling in London?" Jerry asked.

"Yes, we are all set," Romana said. "But you'd better look after my man; I have a lot of fixing up to do round here!"

"Yes m'am, I understand. We'll take real good care of him.

Can I ask just one question of you just now?" Jerry asked. "What's on tonight's menu? I'm kinda starvin'!"

We all laughed. The meal time was going to involve the finer details of the coming weeks. How each of us was to act or talk if we saw Rodrigo or one of his men. Essentially, we were to try to go about our daily lives as normal. Sort the menus, get the best price on the dockside, and fix up the old building. Yes, just business as usual.

CHAPTER EIGHT

Scott phoned and made the arrangement next morning to meet with Rodrigo at the restaurant that evening. He quizzed Scott as to who was to be there. As briefed, Scott said it would be just him and Romana. He had a proposition he wanted to put to him. Rodrigo's curiosity was raised with the tone of his voice and he tried to enquire further.

"Sorry," said Scott. "You will have to wait until tonight. But I think it may well be of interest to you."

Thelma checked the hidden microphones on Scott and Romana were working okay and then they settled themselves upstairs out of sight.

Right on cue Rodrigo arrived at seven thirty for drinks. "Philippe, you look well. Thanks for coming. Romana will be out soon, she has just popped back into the kitchen to check with Enrico everything is under control. Let me get you a drink. What will you have? Wine?"

"Ah yes, wine. I fancy a little red."

"Sorry we don't have any rosé as fine as you have."

"Yes you do, my apologies please, I have left it in my car."

He stood up from the table and waived his arm aloft. The car door opened and his driver came scuttling across the road with a couple of bottles.

"Please, if I may suggest we open just one and then you and the ever gorgeous Romana can have one to yourselves on another occasion. How is that, alright I hope?"

"Well thank you, Philippe, that's a splendid idea. Talking of the gorgeous Romana here she is now. Mind you, Philippe, she has been all afternoon getting ready," laughed Scott.

"Oh Scott, you do exaggerate. I have not been all afternoon. The last two hours I've been in the kitchen sorting out tonight's menu with Enrico. Today's catch was fantastic. We are going to sample, even if I say so myself, the Ocean's Pantry's finest speciality. You brought some of that rosé, Philippe. How kind, thank you. A toast! To new beginnings."

Scott looked at Romana. She seemed to be living the part of mine host a bit too much.

"Excuse me, I need the bathroom." Scott got up and left the table.

A few moments later he was at the kitchen doorway, walking back into the restaurant. "Romana," he beckoned to her. "Enrico has asked you check out this sauce. I would but I only know how to eat it, wouldn't have a clue how to cook it." Romana made her polite 'excuse me' and went to the kitchen passing Scott. "Romana, don't worry, just be you," Scott whispered. "We don't have to work too hard at play acting how we want to befriend him you know?"

"Oh I know but I'm nervous around him. Okay, point taken. Now go, go and sit with him while I sort this sauce."

"Romana, as long as we are together I will never tell you any lies. I hope you remember that and have trust in me. The sauce was just a fib. Give me a kiss and come out in a minute. Relax and just be you. I'll go back to Rodrigo."

"I think Enrico is okay, he is under instructions from Romana to double-check everything. She wants this meal to be something special after that feast you put on for us at that fantastic house of yours."

"You like my house?"

"Of course, who wouldn't? One day I hope to have a house like that. The other thing is the fine art you have. Wow! I know that Jerry guy is into his art stuff, but I can see there's somethin' about it that for me says 'big time', if you know what I mean. Look, we will talk a bit later okay. There is some business I think you might want to discuss with me. But Romana is not to be troubled by any business deals, if you get my meaning?"

"I understand, tonight is to be social subjects only, yes?"

"Well probably till after the coffee is served, that's when I bet she disappears back into the kitchen to check that Enrico is doing the washing up to her liking."

As she emerged again from the kitchen door the two men looked up in her direction from their little huddle. "I am sorry about that, but I just needed to check on the sauce. I know how you like your fish, so tonight we will have the house specialty. The Ocean's Pantry's Seafood Pot, mussel bisque."

The mussels were marinated in garlic for hours previously. It came to the table in an earthenware pot which had been heated through to keep the chowder hot throughout the time it took to eat the mussels before the individual could even start to tuck into the cauldron of seafood within. The chowder contained almost everything that swam off the local shores here. There were prawns, squid, shrimp, crab, tuna and scallops. All of which had been slowing simmering in 'Mama's' secret recipe sauce.

When Romana returned to the table, the two men stood. Rodrigo was quick to offer her a chair. He was always outwardly the gentleman. "Well?" Scott asked.

"All in order, Enrico has done the sauce just as I like. And before you ask, no I will not tell you Mama's secret." A light-hearted chuckle came from Rodrigo and Scott.

The evening meal passed by albeit with some strained pauses in the conversation. There was an air of anticipation present that everyone was experiencing. Romana definitely struggled at times to maintain the charade that she and Scott were trying to uphold. There were even times when Rodrigo faltered in finding something to talk about. But it was he who usually came up with something to say. He was after all good on small talk.

As anticipated on cue, it was during coffee, Romana made her excuses to sort out the kitchen. This was the opportunity for Scott to discuss with Rodrigo his plans to 'get into the BIG league' and make some serious money. After some introductory small talk on the subject, Scott started to talk about his love of the finer things in life.

"I couldn't help but notice some of those works hung on the walls of your house. My trip to Miami proved pretty good and I hope productive."

Rodrigo sat up with renewed interest.

"An old friend of mine has told me of a job I may be interested in. It means I have to go to London some time in the next month or so, and move on to Singapore, then Australia, and back here a few weeks later."

Rodrigo looked pensive as Scott continued.

"Now I'm kinda guessing here, but I think what I am about to tell you, Philippe, you are gonna be interested in and would like to be part of. You know about art, Philippe, I'm saying that because of how you gave us the grand tour the other night. So, you no doubt will have heard about the forthcoming exhibition in London at the Tate?"

"I had heard something," replied Rodrigo rather hesitantly.

Scott continued. "An exclusive display of works that have not only, not seen the public light of day for years, but will not be together again in a public place on display for many more years to come, if at all. There will be a couple of exhibits in this collection of particular interest I feel to you. But there is one piece that I am sure you would just love to have."

"What kind of paintings?" Rodrigo quizzed.

"A Joseph Mallord William Turner and not just any old Turner. But the final painting from his work of ten I believe, the Piazzetta and the Doge's Palace. Correct me if I am wrong, but I also believe that nine of these ten were obtained by, shall we say, less than fair means and are now displayed across the world in private collections? Again, I stress my knowledge is limited on the matter of fine art. But the scene of the 'Grand Canal' at the top of your magnificent staircase looks very familiar to me." Scott quipped, inwardly shaking with nerves. Had he over-stepped the mark and potentially frightened off Rodrigo?

Scott cut the brief awkward silence by coming straight back at Rodrigo. "I have been involved in one or two jobs in Europe which have served me well. But each job is getting harder. Every security system is getting more complex. The risks are getting harder and harder. You can see what I have here with Romana. I don't what to lose that. But, I need just one last job to help set up a new life with her. Anything I earned from previous jobs I have squandered. But not this one, this will be different. Any rewards I get from this will be wisely invested – here with the love of my life."

"You said there were some other pieces? What pieces exactly?" Rodrigo asked in a very straight business-like voice.

"There are a few pieces of porcelain from Italy, Venice to be exact. The majority of them are Francesco Vezzi's work. All of them authenticated to be from 1722. As I'm sure you know that's just a couple of years after he had opened his factory in Venice. Other pieces date back to the Doge era. I wanted to know more. But let's just say at the moment I am on a need to know basis. Then there are some other paintings from Holland. Again, I don't have the exact details just yet, other than to say they are reputed to be priceless. So knowing what I have seen at your place, I was keen to talk with you."

"Scott, what makes you think I would be interested in what

you are telling me? We have only just met. Why do you tell me these things and ask in a roundabout way for money, and more to the point intimate I have gathered my collection by any means other than the open auction houses of the world? If I am not mistaken you are thinking I would be interested in buying these works?"

Rodrigo's tone was soured. Scott felt uneasy and was not sure if he had stepped over the mark and pushed his luck too far in trying to gain Rodrigo's confidence.

"Scott, you are young and ambitious and I do like that in a man. Slightly naïve maybe, but when I was your age I wanted so much more – the finer things that are on offer out there in this big bad world. I yearned for style, class and power. Power to control my own destiny." His soured tone eased to a more relaxed chuckle of a voice. He smirked.

"You have shown trust to me, Scott. Trust is an important thing when dealing in business. You have put your trust in me that I will not to tell the authorities of your plans. So why, I ask myself? Do you want something more of me? Not just the investment to finance this heist, I wonder?"

Scott felt uneasy thinking he had blown it.

"I respect you, Scott, and I think I can trust you. I can certainly help you make a head start, providing of course, that these pieces are what you say they are." His voice lowered again and he continued, "Scott, you need to know, if you try to cross me or deceive me in any way…" he paused. "I will leave it there. I think we understand each other. My only interest is in the 'finer things of life'. I am not interested in you or anything to do with you. Business is business as far as I am concerned. Are we clear on that?"

Scott nodded in agreement. He hadn't until now seen this side of Rodrigo and was inwardly shocked to that end. The bumbling man he had met a couple of nights ago had quite a darker side to his character. He was sure what he had just seen was only a mild example of what could be and it made Scott even more determined that this plan had to work.

"If we are to continue, Scott, I need more information, so where do these pieces come from?" Rodrigo questioned. "I guess from what you tell me they are from a collection?" Rodrigo grinned with an almost devious look. "I think I need to see some proof of their authenticity if I am to do what I think you want me to do. Also, I want to know how they were obtained, where they came from. I have many friends in the art world. Heaven forbid I was to be tangled up in something that involved them. Enlighten me on your part in this and how the pieces can be gotten? The days of getting prizes like this from a museum are long gone. The security available nowadays means next to nothing can be gotten out of those places. No, correct me if I am wrong. But these have come from a private collection haven't they?"

Scott was pleased with the turnaround in Rodrigo's attitude and tone after the earlier dialogue. He was obviously hooked into the thought of getting some more treasure.

"When I was at college I studied science, electrical engineering to be exact. While there I met a guy. He had this absolute fascination for electrical engineering, mechanical engineering and mathematics. You may have heard of him, or at least his father. They are of the same name. Paul Radeon. We have kept in touch on and off ever since."

"Well, well, you mean the Paul Radeon who has gotten into just about every safe known to man?" interrupted Rodrigo.

"Yes, the same Radeon. Now I only ever once met his father when I was there at college. He collected Paul at the end of term one summer. I'll never forget it, it was the first time I had seen a Ferrari. They could hardly get Junior's suitcase in the trunk."

"They spent that summer vacation in Italy together." Rodrigo interrupted again as if like a child listening to a familiar storybook and wanting to show his parent how he was familiar with the outcome of a page in the book.

"Milan, June 1961. A van Gogh is stolen from the national museum. Later that month a collector's house is broken into on the outskirts of Florence. Although the break-in was reported openly the content of the theft was never disclosed."

Rodrigo's knowledge was almost infinite as he described further thefts around the whole country during that summer. Although thoroughly briefed by both Jerry and Thelma, Scott was a little nervous that Rodrigo's knowledge may trip him up. He decided to change tack.

"Yes, I think it's fair to say you are aware of, or even knew, the two Paul Radeons. Paul senior unfortunately is no longer with us. He passed."

Again, Rodrigo cut in to finish the sentence. "It was last March after suffering a heart attack whilst on the Côte d'Azur." It was as if he had studied this man and his activities throughout his life.

"You certainly seem to be familiar with Radeon. You didn't by any chance go to college making him your chosen subject did you?" Scott cut back in with.

"Let's just say that Paul Radeon and I knew of each other. We did some business from time to time. He was a genius when it came to out-smarting the authorities. Definitely the only man I know to crack any safe put before him. Unfortunately, he became greedy. As I said, Scott, do not try to cross me." The scowl in Rodrigo's voice returned momentarily. "Scott, you know his son? So tell me, is he as good?" His tone bounced back again on a lighter vane.

"Oh he's good. Did you read about the Egyptian scriptures taken three years ago from the Cairo national museum? He acquired those to order for a collector in California. By all accounts every conceivable device was used to protect those scriptures from anyone taking them from their display cabinets. He even added one or two pieces by way of a bonus for the Californian. He had gotten him some jewellery from the boy king himself, Tutamkamum. Not a bad bonus heh? Look, Philippe, let me cut to the chase, Romana will be back out here any time. We need to meet, and soon, to discuss what I have in mind and how it's going to work. What about tomorrow morning?"

That was Romana's cue.

Jerry, who had been listening intently to the whole conversation through the hidden microphones, had crept down the stairs to alert Romana to get back out into the restaurant with the two men.

"Hello again you two, I got carried away with clearing up. I sent Enrico home, he has done such a good job tonight for all our customers. Anyway, I thought you two would want to talk men's talk so I left you to it."

Some more small talk took place but it was very apparent that the evening was over. Rodrigo summoned his car which had been waiting just across the road from the restaurant on the quayside. The driver, who had been slumped behind the steering wheel in the driver's seat, quickly straightened himself up and jumped out to open the rear door of the car. Rodrigo crossed the road with both Scott and Romana a pace behind him. He shook Scott by the hand. He then turned to Romana with his arms outstretched placing his hands on her shoulders. "My dear, as ever a wonderful meal and such beautiful company. Good evening to you both." He kissed her on both cheeks and turned to his car. Romana glanced quickly at Scott with a worried expression, frowning slightly. Had Scott got a decision from Rodrigo whilst she was in the kitchen? Scott also had a frown as well as a sinking feeling right to the pit of his stomach. Despite all of the planning, all of the briefings with Thelma and Jerry, the opportunity had gone. There had been no sign or indication that Rodrigo was interested. That was it. The gleaming monster of a car with its sleek running boards and bulbous front wheel arches fired into life. Rodrigo could not been seen through the darkened rear windows. The car pulled away. Walking back across the road in silence, the few paces seemed like a mile. The car turned a couple of hundred yards down the harbour-side road where it was wider. Scott, with a reassuring arm around Romana's shoulder, stopped and turned again to bid their guest goodbye. The car approached slowly and stopped beside them at the entrance of the Ocean's Pantry. Some ten seconds passed. The two of them again frowned but whilst looking were almost hypnotised by the beast of the car now just purring directly in front of them. The reflection of their faces on the rear window glass disappeared as the glass slowly eased down into a huge slab of bullet-proof armour that was the door. Although sat in the back, Rodrigo could not been seen by the two of them. Such was the size of the car which no doubt dated back to the Al Capone era, quite in keeping with Rodrigo's ego. A hand appeared on the door frame and leaning forward with a welcoming expression on his face, Rodrigo gestured to them both. His speech slightly slurred.

"Scott, why don't you come up to the house tomorrow morning, if you are not too busy that is? I will personally show you around the estate. Romana, that will be alright with you will it not?"

Turning to Romana, Scott asked her with an almost excited tone to his voice. The weight of disappointment had all of a sudden been lifted from his shoulders and just as quickly the feeling in his stomach had gone from one of anguish and almost nausea to one of contentment from the hearty meal they had had only a half hour ago.

"Romana, you okay with that? I'm sure the estate and all its farming doesn't hold much interest for you?"

"Oh no, it's not really my thing. With the greatest respect, Philippe."

"Romana, darling I fully understand what you mean. Scott, shall we say around ten? I will send my driver to pick you up here."

"That would be great; the ride in your car is, I have to say, somewhat smoother than Romana's jeep, with the greatest of respect of course." He gestured and joked toward Romana.

Bidding them both farewell until tomorrow, Rodrigo's car disappeared toward the headland road.

"Well, I don't know what made him change his mind but it's safe to say he bought it, lock, stock and barrel. Let's just hope I can build on that tomorrow morning. Hi Jerry, get everything you want?" Having watched the car move off from the restaurant from the upstairs Jerry was now shaking Scott firmly by the hand.

"Sure did. Now I suggest you have an early night. I want to meet you here at seven to cover the London job again so you don't trip up on any point. Rodrigo has had first-hand experience of some of those Radeon jobs. He will want to know the exact detail to the enth degree, I'm sure. C'mon, let's call it a day."

CHAPTER NINE

Seven came around all too quickly. Jerry and Scott got straight to it over the coffee that Romana had had on the go since six thirty. She had been awake long before daybreak anticipating the morning meeting between Scott and Rodrigo. Jerry was in his element, now going into the detail of just about everything Scott would need to know with absolute military precision.

"Scott, every which way you look at it, Rodrigo will want to know 'how' and 'why'. Just put yourself in his shoes for a minute. You'd want to know wouldn't you?"

"Well yes, I guess you're right. What about the payment particulars?" Scott asked. "How do I quantify the price? If the Doge Palace painting is priceless, then how much do I want for it?"

Jerry had an informative expression on his face not dissimilar to that of a school master contemplating a question from a student.

"Quite simply, everything has a value, whether it's tea, coffee, sugar or even cocaine. The painting's value or price has to be like any other commodity, cover its cost price value to get it to market. But of course, then with the added on profit margin the seller is looking to make. But when it comes to art, profits can be high for the seller, beyond their wildest expectations. Why? Simply because some of the buyers are addicted as we said before. Some will pay way over the odds just to stop someone else getting a piece. Pathetic really, just like spoilt kids sometimes. Rodrigo for instance will certainly know his. He will know his production cost price, and of course he will know how much he can sell it for to get a good margin when selling direct into the drugs arena. But here, this deal is different. He has to weigh up how much you will want to offset your fixed costs of getting the art from the Tate and he will also have an idea of how much gear you will want to convert into a handsome profit. Obviously the profit has to be factored in as well. The paintings cost price has to cover paying off our inside man, hiring the trucks, accommodation along the route, etc. etc. you name it. Everything that costs a dime to a dollar has to be accounted for. This is just regular business, the same as baking a loaf in a bakery. You gotta pay for the flour before you make the bread. No pun intended. Rodrigo knows the costs involved believe me; he has had 'works' from Europe before."

Jerry covered again and again the infinite detail that hopefully would cover any question asked of Scott. Scott in turn would respond by replying in what would seem a second nature confident manner. They rehearsed for the couple of hours they had before Scott was due to be picked up. What was the price of all this hard work? The planning, the transport, the bribes, you name it, all that was needed to bring this guy down amounted to close on three million US dollars, or certainly the equivalent value in cocaine. If Rodrigo agreed to the deal the FBI could charge and arrest him on two counts. Receiving stolen works of art and dealing in narcotics.

I arrived just before Rodrigo's car pulled up outside the restaurant. Scott sat nervously at one of the tables to the front of restaurant sipping a coffee. Apart from gesturing to him a quick kind of hello when I pulled up, we didn't speak. There was an air of understandable tension given the circumstances which could unfold with regrettable results.

Grabbing my tools from out back, I made the token effort of fixing a dripping tap in the main kitchen sink, from here I could almost see straight out to the quayside. Although I had removed the tap body my mind, and indeed eye, was fixed on what was happening regarding Scott. The car arrived right on cue demonstrating yet again Rodrigo's precise time-keeping. One thing about him despite all of his foibles and traits, he was always punctual. That included everything within his control. Whether it was the farm estate or something as simple as arranging a lift back to his house. Scott waived to Romana and me with Jerry staying right out of sight. Jerry thought as a precaution the less he and Thelma were seen at the Ocean's Pantry by Rodrigo or anyone to do with him, the better.

We busied ourselves around the restaurant but it is fair to say our thoughts were elsewhere, thinking of Scott. During this time no-one spoke and a strange atmosphere fell on the normally light-hearted and uplifting ambience that is the Ocean's Pantry. I phoned Sam and arranged to see him later at the Kubota Plaza Hotel. He like me would want to see Rodrigo finally have his comeuppance once and for all. What seemed like days later, Scott was getting out of the Chevrolet with all its gleaming chrome glinting in the mid-afternoon sun. There from the curves of this rounded metal monster emerged the broadest smirk from his well-chiselled jaw line. "Unless I am mistaken I have just hooked one of the biggest fish in the bay!" Until now we had acknowledged his return but had carried on doing our chores. There was me sweeping the floor, Romana laying up the tables for dinner and clearing away the remnants of the few tourists who had been in for lunch.

She ran arms outstretched, jumping into his. I shook his hand. "We must phone Jerry and Thelma."

"No need, we're here. We saw the car go past our hotel."

Scott told us everything – how Rodrigo had quizzed him on how, when, and of course, why. He did agree the price but he also took some persuading as firstly he thought three million was pretty high, but then he would, wouldn't he? I guess the same would have been said if it had only been one million, but that was Rodrigo all over.

Scott said how he justified the costs to him to get the job even started. At this point Rodrigo had offered to pay Scott some set-up money to help him speed things up. Scott had told him he couldn't get things off the ground just yet due to a lack of funds. Now he was in pocession of $100,000 in cash to pay some of the securities further down the line.

Rodrigo was as keen as mustard. He wanted the Turner probably more than the others pieces. So did it mean this particular painting would complete his collection? Could this be the one missing from the eight taken from the collection some twenty years previously? Jerry and Thelma certainly thought so. It did seem that way. Any tenacious man with the character of Rodrigo would not part with a hundred thousand dollars despite his polite words of helping a young man get started in life towards having the better things as he enjoyed. Rodrigo was too much of a selfish man for that.

So, the trap was set. Jerry got on with things straightaway. Certain arrangements were already in place, as had been the case for the last few years in an effort to nail and pin down Rodrigo once and for all. Thelma had said when we first met and exposed ourselves to each other that the FBI had had Rodrigo in their sights for years. The two of them went back to the hotel to make a start. The plan was to alert their bosses 'it was on'! In turn their colleagues would go to Europe to discuss with the Tate what exhibits were to be shipped to them and when, but the Tate would not be aware of the heist that was about to take place. As far as the Tate was concerned the Americans were dealing with bringing together a collection from across Europe for them to show for a month. This was to be a unique opportunity for everyone who was an art fanatic to see so many Masters in one place. Possibly never to be seen again in the gallery in London or come to that, in any public venue in the future. The next couple of days were going to be unusual to say the least.

Over the next few days, Scott and Jerry spent more time together working out the exact detail of what was to happen in London. The National Gallery was to hold an exhibition with works by artists from around Europe. In particular some paintings by two Dutch artists, Jan Vermeer and Jacob Isaakszoon van Ruisdael. Thelma explained to Romana and me about these artists, their lives and their importance within the art world. Both painted in and around the mid-seventeenth century. The work included in the main day-to-day street scenes, but more importantly landscapes. One of van Ruisdael's pupils from that time was Meindert Hobbema. He in turn painted landscapes which greatly influenced the English artists such as Constable and Gainsborough. Either way, van Ruisdael's work is sought after and held in high regard, let alone high value as well. This exhibition is to have some of the works from the leading Dutch artists from this era. Rembrandt and William Kalf, who had done a few 'still life' pieces, Albert Cuyp and Russdael who specialized in landscapes as well. This was the first time such a gathering of these famous Dutch works had been brought together in one place. There was also to be some works that for the last twenty or so years had been kept away from public view having been held in private collections.

The landscapes were what clinched it for Rodrigo, from what Scott had said. The Turner especially, but just as keen was he to get his hands on one of the Dutch works. Certainly his collection seemed to be in the main, landscapes.

Life and the daily routine remained the same for Romana and me over the next few days. Scott met up with Rodrigo from time to time to keep the relationship alive.

On the fourth day the afternoon was sort of surreal and passed slowly. It soon changed though when Jerry announced, "It was on!" Although we all wanted to have justice for what Rodrigo had had a hand in, there was an air of trepidation and anticipation. Despite what was now beginning to unfold, did any of us really want to be part of it?

CHAPTER TEN

The plan started to become a reality. Jerry and Thelma would leave the day after tomorrow on an early morning boat to the neighbouring island of Manacor, where a seaplane would fly them to the capital. Here their FBI colleagues would meet with them and they would fly into Miami for a brief stopover before flying on to New York.

Basing themselves in the Big Apple, they would oversee and co-ordinate the initial setting up of the operation from there. When the heist was to happen they would move to London. Their job would also involve clearing up the mess and confusion that would surely prevail when it was made public knowledge of the ferry 'hit'.

I left the restaurant around five and headed back down the headland road to home. What was this feeling? I asked myself. Was I happy? Was I nervous or unsure? Truthfully, I felt a combination, I guess.

After a nap I showered and made my way back to town to meet with Sam as arranged in the hotel bar. Already sitting at my usual corner table, Sam had a couple of beers in front of him. "Thought I'd set them up. No rum tonight though. I'm under strict orders from that girl of yours." He beamed. It was strange. I had never heard anyone refer to Romana as 'that girl of yours'. Even Sam knew it hit the right nerve for me. I shook his hand but not as I would usually shake his hand when we met each time as was always the case. But this time I held on to it. "Thank you, my friend."

A momentary silence between us was broken when he

replied slowly and very exactly. "You are very welcome my friend." Almost telepathically Sam knew our meeting was more than our usual get together. We discussed what was about to happen. Albeit we spoke quietly as we couldn't be sure as to who might be listening. Although with the music booming I am sure even if we had shouted out in distress, no one would have come to our rescue, let alone could they have heard our mutterings. I knew I could trust Sam not to say a word to a soul. Come to think of it, I would trust him with my life such was our friendship. After all he was with me on that fateful night all those years ago. No, he like me wanted Rodrigo brought to justice.

We only had just a few beers – as I had promised Romana. I would not be stupid and drink too much, so as planned I got back to the Ocean's Pantry before it shut. Briefly catching sight of Romana in the kitchen I gestured 'hello' and pointed skyward to indicate I was going to bed. My room for this evening was the small single guest room which looked out the harbour and quayside.

Despite my initial thoughts of a couple of days ago, the time had flown by. Scott and Romana spent the little free time they had together quizzing each other on every move, every detail of names, places and the history that surrounded the forthcoming Tate job. Although the actual job would not happen for six weeks from now their time was some-what sporadic. It was key that life continued as routinely as possible. Thelma had made us well aware and told us, "You cannot trust anyone but yourselves from now till Rodrigo is put away. He could have any of his heavies, men or women, out to gain information on any of us. He would definitely be on a high alert because he didn't trust anyone, especially where money – and his money at that – was at stake!"

Thelma and Jerry's last night dinner was a fairly quiet affair before their departure the next morning. Conversation was subdued, polite small talk amongst the five of us. It was fair to say everyone was slightly anxious. We just wanted to get things going.

With two weeks to go, Scott left for the States. Needless to say it was a tearful departure. I stopped over again at the restaurant the night before so I could bid him farewell before his six o'clock boat for Manacor which then tied in with the early flight out of there. He would be dining alone tonight in Miami. Jerry had arranged a direct flight then on to London two days later.

Scott's London base was somewhere around the Fulham area. A place I had fond memories of but no doubt like so much in my life, things had moved on or changed beyond our memories of them. For me the knowledge of what was about to happen next was somewhat vague. The FBI thought it best for all of us who remained here in South America, for it to be on a 'need to know' basis only. The least we knew the better, as a precaution against the heist not working entirely to plan. It goes without saying that we all desperately wanted to know the exact detail to the 'enth' degree of what Scott had to do or was actually doing at any given time whilst he was away. But of course, on hindsight it made perfect sense to us all not to know.

Romana and I were to have no contact with Scott until he called us. The one call he did make was brief, the night he arrived in Miami. It was really just to say all was well, albeit the flight was a little bumpy. Miami was humid as usual and the noise of traffic after the peaceful weeks spent with us would take some getting used to. That was the last time we heard his voice for some three weeks.

Jerry had arranged for a woman, Brenda, to call the Ocean's Pantry and speak to Romana on a weekly basis. She would update Romana in a convoluted way, sort of code-like, in order to tell her of Scott's well-being. This again, another precaution the FBI had insisted on. If any of Rodrigo's people got suspicious or tapped the phone the ruse was that Brenda and her brother had stayed at the restaurant a few months ago and had struck up a good friendship with Romana. She would in fact probably return for a short visit with her brother in another couple of months' time. Needless to say Brenda's supposed brother was Scott.

CHAPTER ELEVEN

A week went by and the tourist numbers declined as is always the way at this time of year. The weather was still good but by three most afternoons the sky would cloud up following the increasing wind. A sharp monsoon-like rain storm would hammer down for half an hour or so clearing the air that had grown heavy in humidity by lunch time. The evenings were spent looking out to the headland watching the setting sun. I remember the first time I saw this sight. I was with Romana's mother. She told me to, "Absorb its natural beauty and remind yourself of the day you had just enjoyed and look forward to the next which may also bring happiness, but more importantly, contentment. Be content."

Quite ironically one evening Romana had asked me, "Are you content, Uncle Joe?"

"Honestly?" I replied.

"Yes of course," she quipped.

"No not quite. The last piece of the jigsaw in my life is missing. It's the piece Rodrigo took. The thing is he hasn't really got that piece to give back to me. But he did have it and he took it from me. When Scott is back here with you and this mess is all cleared up, ask me then. We will all stand here; watch the sun go down just like this. Ask me then."

She linked her arm in mine and rested her head on my shoulder. We stood in silence, our gaze fixed on the sinking sun whose glow and heat were extinguished by the sea. Over our shoulder the new moon took over as the dominant feature of the sky.

"Why don't we get Scott to play his guitar or the piano at sunset? It might bring in a few more customers, don't you think?" Romana asked.

"Are you sure it won't turn them away? I have heard him sing as well you know!" She smacked my arm in jest.

"Who can I get to tune up that old piano though?"

"I will ask Sam. They have some chap who has been coming to the hotel to do theirs for years from Manacor, I think. I'll look in to it. He might do a deal if he has two pianos to tune on the same trip over here. We'll see."

Brenda's phone call six days later to Romana told her that the trip was to be delayed as her brother was called away unexpectedly on business in Europe. But all was well regarding their return trip to the Ocean's Pantry. They would want two rooms as before but now in five weeks' time. This in fact corresponded with the time-frame Jerry had told us before he left. Based on this call the schedule was running to plan. Scott had obviously been in London for a couple of days, probably getting over his jet lag. Then he was now somewhere in Europe which meant he and the team would be preparing to round up the various works.

Brenda would call again with coded messages within her conversation over the next couple of weeks – like how her brother had been out shopping for new clothes which he detested, for the meetings he had to make with new clients in various cities across Europe. Also, how he loved all the different cars and trucks he was seeing and how he had singled out his favourite. What this really meant was that all the 'works' had been gathered together and their departure times were now in place ready for the off. The transport was also sorted by the reference to him having 'singled out' a car. It was for sure Scott had not 'singled out' a car for himself whilst in Europe unless it was a Ferrari or Porsche. He liked his big American Chevys and Pontiacs too much to want any kind of European runabout.

I had to assure Romana after each call that although right here, right now, life did not seem good and there was still a way to go, all would come good for us. "It won't be that long before you ask me if I am content."

Out of the blue one sunny afternoon around three, Romana and I were tidying the front of house tables from lunch. The quiet was broken by the sound of a woman shouting, it was coming from across the road on the quayside.

"Hey! Hey, can I get a room here?!" A couple of cars went past before we could see it was Thelma. She crossed to us. "Sure hope the house special is on the menu tonight?" Never quiet was Thelma.

"What are you doing here? Where is Jerry?" Romana asked.

"Oh he's away on business in New York. I had some vacation time owing to me from work to use up, so what better place to go where the rooms are good, the food fabulous and the company like family? Not a hard choice I would say! So, here I am!"

"Your case, where is your luggage?" I asked.

"Oh, it's across the street, I was just wanting to hug you guys I forgot all 'bout it. That's me, see what I want and just go for it. My daddy always used to say I was too impetuous. Like I say, if I wants somethin' I just go get it. I could always get some more clothes if someone has taken the case. But to see you two at that moment without waiting another minute or even second by picking up the case? Well you couldn't get that minute or second back, replace it. C'mon, can I get a quick freshen up and a drink?"

Romana hugged her again. "Oh it is so good to see you. Of course, follow me. Room two is ready. You can have that one overlooking the front. But first, tell me all, and I mean all, is it all okay?" There was a certain waiver in Romana's voice at this point.

Thelma smiled at her, spoke quietly and reassuringly. "I promise it could not be better." Romana sighed with relief and smiled. "When Jerry said he would take care of him he meant it. Officially I shouldn't tell you this, but as a woman talking to another woman, he has people watching his every move. He wouldn't know it mind you. But that is done for his protection so he continues to act naturally. Well, as natural as is possible under the circumstances. You can bet Rodrigo has people watching him but obviously for very different reasons. They will want to know he is doing what he said he would do, especially as he already has some of Rodrigo's money to set things up with."

Thelma hugged Romana again with an almost maternal manner despite the two women being of a similar age. In a slightly louder than a whisper, she broke the silence.

"Enough already, show me this room, I want ten minutes to freshen up then I'll come back downstairs for a drink. Hey Joe, on my reckoning that will be long enough to chill a good rosé don't you think? Before you say anything, yes you have." She handed me a bottle from her holdall. "Get it in the fridge, I'll be down in ten!" I followed the pair of them upstairs carrying Thelma's case. Romana opened up the door to the guest room which overlooked the front. Putting the case on the bed I went back down.

Romana came down and went straight in to see Enrico, asking him to get a house special on the go. "He's going to be okay isn't he, Uncle Joe?" She looked lifted again, something I had not seen since Scott's departure. She wasn't exactly down as such, just she had been a little subdued. Thelma's visit was just the boost she wanted.

I have to say, and not as a lover of too much wine, the rosé was a very palatable. Thelma told me her visit was planned to reassure us that all was going to plan. She was also to try and get any information on what Rodrigo was up to. What was being said around the town if anything? It was no secret that some of his henchmen had a loose tongue on occasion around the smaller back street bars of the town. Sam and I were to take Thelma out one night on a bar crawl to see if we could glean any local knowledge. But tonight we were to tuck into the house special and relax.

As planned, two nights later, Sam and I arrived at the restaurant just after nine and met up with Thelma ready for our bar crawl-come-fact-finding expedition. Romana decided to join us as well as there were very few left in the restaurant and they were nearly finished. Enrico assured her he could clear up and lock up as usual.

Our first stop off on the regular tourist trail was the Mistral Bar. This was mainly frequented by the local fishermen, all of whom were known to us. They did look a little surprised to see us in their bar though. Well not so much Sam and I, but certainly the two women. We found ourselves at the bar chatting and joking with the crew of the Starfish. It had only been a few hours earlier when Romana was on the quayside haggling with Miguel the captain for a deal on his catch. In the corner of the bar were a couple of guys who seemed to be keeping themselves to themselves. Maybe I was just being paranoid. Thelma cleverly asked the men if 'life for them was still the same old relaxed pace' she had come to notice and enjoy on her previous visits. They didn't answer and just shunned her presence at their table.

"So, from what you are saying, nothing too exciting happening around here then?" she asked.

At this point our two friends got up and left but not without giving our small group a sideways glance. Perhaps there was more to them than we first thought. Thelma shrugged her shoulders and walked back to all of us at the bar.

"Strange guys, you ever seen them before?" she asked the group as a whole. Everyone sort of shook their heads in a collective 'No'. Again she shrugged her shoulders. Something had registered with her as she turned towards the door to watch them leave. Drinking up we went further away from the waterfront and into a bar even Sam and I would normally steer clear of. The Mermaid's Resting Place, it had always been somewhat of a den of doom and gloom. Even when I first came to this part of the world, and worst still in my darkest period, I would rarely drink here. Like an infamous Western movie, the place fell silent when we walked in. After an awkward pause the barman, Mario Rodrigo spoke.

"Long time no see, Sam, Joe. What's your poison? And your friends, what'll they have?"

We just ordered beers. Looking around our two as yet un-introduced 'new friends' were surprisingly sitting in the corner. The head of the beers had just been supped. Thelma was the first to speak breaking the by now un-comfy atmosphere.

"So! This is a real local bar? I bet if these walls could talk there would be a tale or two to tell."

There was a distinct mumbling from around the bar but nothing that was audible.

"Senor Rodrigo here is Philippe's brother, isn't that right, Mario?" I asked.

"Si! Not that you would think looking at my humble bar and knowing what he owns. But at least I worked for what I have here honestly!"

"Oh dear Mario, I can call you Mario? I am Thelma." He nodded his head in approval.

"I sense there is no love lost between you two then?" Our friends in the corner disappeared into the toilets.

"Are they new in town or just in here?" Sam asked Mario.

"Don't know. They've been coming in just over the last few weeks. They don't say much. Just have a few beers and go each night around eleven. Tried to chat to them, ya know? I need to know who is coming into my bar. I don't want any trouble."

I glanced at my watch, it was almost eleven. They came out, drank their beer and left, again giving us all a kind of threatening stare, stern at the very least. "You see? They are trouble. I know that look!" Mario muttered.

"Why did you say what was here was gotten honestly compared to your brother, Mario? I've met Philippe a few times, he seems okay to me," Thelma said trying to get more than just a few syllables out of Mario.

"Lady, you don't want to know!"

"Try me, Mario, I love a good story of intrigue and adventure."

"Joe, Sam, you know what I mean," Mario replied

"Hey, he's your brother, Mario. No I'll leave you to tell Thelma here what he's like," I replied

"Well, Mario, I guess it's down to you then," Thelma quipped.

"Well where do I start?" It was an unusual twist given the atmosphere that had greeted us. It was as if Mario had all this frustration that involved Philippe for years bottled up inside him. It could now finally be released and vented like some kind of gushing volcano spewing all this information and hatred out.

He talked how as kids Philippe, who was older by some twelve years, had always had a chip on his shoulder when it came to Mario as a brother. Philippe had to have the upper hand in everything. He would tease Mario about the smallest of things. How it was that their parents bought him clothes as new but Mario only ever had the hand-me-downs. So it went on with similar stories of the love-hate relationship Philippe and Mario had shared. The feeling was mutual. Mario as a teen and even as a young man in his twenties would challenge Philippe regarding the company he was keeping, but their father would back Philippe saying Mario was over reacting and needed to toughen up like his brother. By the time Mario was thirty he and Philippe hardly ever spoke to each other. They might pass a cursory 'Hello' if they met in the town but that was all. When their parents had passed away Mario had bought the bar here having worked on the fishing boats and saving hard the little he earned. Even at the time of the reading of their parents will, Philippe had a few sarcastic remarks aimed at Mario. It was as if Philippe had been born an adult having no association with their parents, not taking stock of the fact that it was their father who had built up the business from a couple of acres of farm land into the vast estate it had become. On reflection, Mario said how just about everything he could remember about Philippe was as if Philippe himself thought it was his God-given right to have it. He couldn't think of one single thing Philippe had genuinely earned or worked for. It had all been given to him on a plate, a silver plate at that.

That said, Mario was no pushover or picture of innocence. He too had a bit of a reputation in his own right. Completely innocent he was not. But I guess running a bar that is frequented by men who enjoy a drink and share different opinions, you need to be strong minded when sorting out a bar room brawl as was often the case in the Mermaid's Resting Place. The passing clientele of sailors and fishermen are a hardy lot who like to express themselves with fists or a chair rather than the gentlemanly approach of discussion or debate. Sharing his knowledge of his brother's wealth was enlightening as well.

I have to say it was all I could do to stop myself from telling Mario what was planned for his dear brother. There was such an air of trust there because of how open he had been talking to us. Speaking later, Sam too had had the same thought cross his mind. Thelma commented how relieved she was to hear that we had given thought to it rather than spurt out the operation details, no matter how small, to Mario. He would have no doubt questioned us further which would have jeopardized everything that was now well in place. Based on our temptation to confide in him, she made us promise not to have anything to do with Mario until his brother was safely locked up behind bars and the key had been thrown away.

"You haven't seen him for years until tonight, so there's no need to try and rekindle a relationship now. Just a few more weeks and you can go there every night of the week if you want!" said Thelma, giving us all something to think about just how serious all of this was.

"Maybe you can go there once in a while but certainly NOT every night!" Romana cut in.

The following afternoon I was sat on my porch looking out to sea. I couldn't help but think that my world of peace and calm might be shattered again as it was when I first arrived back home from the mess that was World War Two. This time though the disruption was to be within my control. Although there were to be some drastic changes to things initially in my life, all would become complete again once the dust had settled.

Life around here would change for not just me, but for quite a few others as well. Romana, Scott and I would get to know each other much more. I guess Jerry and Thelma will leave to be assigned to another case somewhere in the world – somewhere where yet another Rodrigo is operating. But the main change of life will come to those who work for Philippe Rodrigo. All the staff that work up at the house and out on the estate. What will happen to them I wonder? Then there are the 'henchmen'. Not that I worry too much for them. Hopefully the FBI can pin something on them as well.

Certainly the locals in town will not miss them. Whenever they came into town they would throw their weight around. Some of the fishermen will be glad to see the back of them. For now though, I sit here watching the glistening water sparkle as bright as diamonds skimming across the waves. The young lads are coming now. The surf is getting up as it does every afternoon. You know how despite all that might be about to happen, life just doesn't get any better than this!

"Hey Joe, are you out back?" I heard Thelma call from the front of the bungalow.

"Yea c'mon round," I shouted back. "I thought I heard a car. How are you?"

"I'm doin' just fine. Thought I'd stop by. I'm here to say my farewells. My work here is done as they say. The Bureau wants me on another job, in Europe this time. Kinda ironic I guess, seeing how all the action from this one will be goin' on at the same time just a few hundred miles away from where I have been assigned.

"Oh no, I thought you would be here for the duration and close by?"

"No, sorry it doesn't work that way. Me and Jerry we are like salesmen. We find out what you want and try to sell to you by closing the deal. You see with us, Jerry and me find out what people have and what would they like. Then knowing this, we put together a game plan to close the deal. Except in our line of business, closing a deal means making an arrest. Again, just like in some businesses, some guys seek out the new potential clients, ask the right questions, then someone else comes in to 'close' the deal. We seek the 'new' business; ask the questions based on our knowledge of the art world. Others 'close' based on our information.

"So right now my work here is done. Jerry will liaise with the 'closers' regarding London. Then he will join me in..." she paused momentarily. "Let's just say you are on a need to know basis here. Sorry Joe, although we have come to be close friends, you, Romana and Scott, there are some things I can't tell you, and my next job is just that." Her tone was somewhat official and formal as if she was now at a first meeting towing the company line. That said, her usual light-hearted tone soon returned.

"Will you be back?" I questioned.

"You try and keep me away! I want to see you keep this place tidy. Then I reckon there will be the wedding!" She laughed.

"Are you sure about that?" I asked.

"Joe, I might be a Federal Agent but underneath the dark suits, Ray-Bans and black shoes I am still a woman ya know. Believe me, Joe, there will be a wedding. Just as soon as Scott is back, you mark my words. So you had better start dusting off your old suit and tie, my man!"

Leaping forward in my mind and dreaming of that picture I felt an air of calm. I pondered the thought for a few seconds.

"Oh I'm sorry, would you like a drink of coffee, juice or beer?"

"Well it's nearly five o'clock, or it will be in an hour or two. Either way, if not here it is somewhere, so a beer would be good. Oh and Joe, a bottle will be just fine. I wouldn't want you in there trying to find a clean glass or at least one without a chip in it!" She laughed

"I'll be right back, two beers comin' up," I said. "There you go," I said handing over the beer. She was leaning against the balcony balustrade just as I had been looking out to sea.

"Thanks. You asked me if I would be back. Well, looking at the view why wouldn't I want to come back? Ya know my job takes me all over the world and I am real lucky to see some beautiful places. But here, here there ain't just a view, it comes with, I don't know, a sort of 'air', an atmosphere of contentment." She turned to where I was now sitting on my rocker. "You know what I mean?" I just raised my bottle of beer, smiled and nodded an approving 'yes'.

"I'm gonna miss you, Thelma. I gotta say I didn't know what to make of you when you and Jerry first arrived. But your knowledge of art is something else. But tell me, does your dad really 'wheel and deal' in art?" She sat down next to me and gently pushed the floor to start the rocker swinging.

"He sure does. Ever since I can remember, that's all he would talk to me about. I love it. You see when I'm talking about it; it's as if my dad is here with me even though I'm thousands of miles away from him. But I genuinely like art anyway. To think sometimes how someone sat down in a studio a couple of hundred years ago and produced works like that using primitive oils and having poor lighting to contend with, it's truly amazing!"

Just for a moment it was as if Thelma was opening up with her affection and emotions, but just as quickly she changed the conversation. "But, as I said, I will be leaving in a couple of days. So I have already spoken to Romana. We are to have a farewell dinner tomorrow night at the Ocean's Pantry. You will come won't you?"

"Try to stop me. I do hope you will keep in touch with us here in this little piece of paradise. Although I was just thinking before you came, not all is too much like paradise right now!" I shrugged.

"Oh it will be and not too long from now, you wait and see," she answered in an assuring tone. "Any chance of a refill?"

"Sure, coming right up!"

"You have got to have one of the best views in the world here, Joe. I don't just mean the view out there across the beach either. I mean your whole view of life. Take my word for it, Joe, keep hold of it and savour it. There are millions who would give anything for what you have here. The next few weeks are just a small blip in the bigger scheme of things!"

As I came back through to the veranda Thelma was swinging back and forth on the rocker. I timed the movement of the swinging hammock just right and eased myself back on to it.

"Here's that beer. Yes I know. Sometimes I pinch myself to remind me I'm not dreaming. I guess if I'd stayed at home in England I would be retired now, worn out having worked in some dead-end hum drum job that I had done since the war, day after grey day taking every grinding monotonous day as it came not really knowing what the big bad world had to offer. You're right, look at me. Life is pretty good. Hell! Finish your beer; let's go surfin' with the boys out there!" I laughed out loud adding, "Don't worry Thelma, life's good but it ain't that good. Even I know my limitations. Let's just watch them for now."

"You're on. You had me worried then, I was beginning to think this wasn't your first beer of the day! Any ways, I'm a girl from the centre of Texas. Joe, I ain't no Californian 'surfer' girl!" She linked her arm in mine as we sipped our beers and looked again out to the horizon.

"Thank you, Joe, from the minute I met you I knew you were a genuine and honest man. I don't get to see that in the majority of people I usually come across."

"You're welcome!" I said in a mocking American accent.

We watched the activities on the beach and out to sea more or less in silence, arms linked for at least half an hour, only un-linking them to have a sip of beer. The breeze got stronger around four as usual and the youngsters started to thin out on the beach and headed home. Thelma reminded me to have faith and patience. All would work out and come good. She left at six saying she would see me tomorrow night at the restaurant; her day would be just mooching around the town and packing her bags. I spent the evening cleaning through the bungalow; it was less effort in the cooler evening temperature than what could be the searing daytime heat. Also, the breeze helped blow the dust up and out of the place. This new found discipline which I had must say had come to be almost therapeutic for me. Doing laundry was still a real chore though. So I employed the services of the laundry in the old town for this. Romana had offered but I didn't want to impose this on her. In any case, I wanted to demonstrate to her that my new found lifestyle included some discipline again. It gave me more work as well. Albeit odd jobs. It was a trade-off at the launderette. I did the odd bit of day to day maintenance either at the shop or at Senorita Chiquita's house. It suited me just fine. I was more at home doing some painting or fixing a shelf than standing at a wash tub knee deep in dirty clothes and soap suds, let alone doing any ironing.

Spending the evening at home I just chilled out pondering over what Thelma had said and how it would all click into place for the better.

The sun rose brightly over the headland. I fired up the old jeep and took my familiar commute to town. A route I had taken now for many a year, but after yesterday's conversation with Thelma I drove it with renewed vigour taking notice of the scenery I had more or less taken for granted.

Romana nodded to me, her hands full with fresh clean tablecloths. Enrico was busy as usual behind her in the kitchen.

"What's to do then?" I asked.

"The sink in the Ladies is blocked, so a lady told me last night, oh and that tap is dripping again," Romana replied.

I set to at once in the Ladies washroom. The afternoon passed by quickly as I sorted a couple of doors upstairs that needed adjusting slightly. Freshening up upstairs I got ready for dinner. Thelma arrived around seven; Romana had the meal ready an hour later. We had a drink as we sat at our table outside in the front corner under the canopy. Thelma told us how all was on schedule in Europe. She had spoken with Jerry last night for an update. All the works were in place for collection and Scott had the transport organized. She obviously reassured Romana he was good and was being watched by some of the best in the business.

Out of the blue Rodrigo's car pulled up across from us on the quayside. Getting out he gave us no time to fathom out what he might be here for. "This could be awkward," I quietly said to Thelma.

"Oh I don't know, more like interesting."

A moment later she greeted him, "Hello, Philippe. How are you?" she confidently asked.

"Good, good. I heard you were in town and thought I must come and say hello. How long are you here for?"

"It is a flying visit, I just took a couple of days right at the last minute. I had some extra vacation time owing to me, plus I left some jewellery here on my last time. So I thought I would kill two birds with one stone. Just a long weekend really, I fly back in a couple of days."

"Philippe, would you like to join us for dinner? I can get another place laid up, it is no problem," Romana asked. Crossing my fingers in my pocket he gave the answer I was hoping for.

"No, no thank you. I have already eaten at home. I am going to my brother's for a drink, but thought whilst I am here in town I must come and at least say hello and goodbye, as it were. Anyway, it is lovely to see you again albeit very briefly, Thelma. I will see you again perhaps?" He pecked her on the back of her hand.

"Oh I'm sure we will see each other again, Philippe." He paused thoughtfully then gestured to us all and crossed back across the road as quickly as he had arrived.

"Well, he doesn't speak to his brother for years, we show up there and Philippe follows. A bit ominous don't you think?" I asked.

"Maybe, he certainly is well informed about who goes where and who talks to whom," Thelma replied.

Thelma's 'vacation' had come to an end all too quickly. The couple of days she did have were spent just doing what most tourists here do. Take a boat ride along the coast and stop off for an afternoon at one of the many quiet little coves or head out of the town to the beach by my place. To be honest that is all you can do, oh except play golf if you stay up at the Kumota Plaza Hotel.

Thelma reassured Romana and me about the operation involving Scott.

"Six weeks from now he will be sitting here with you and I bet given a week or two after that you will wish he was out from under your feet!"

Her taxi was waiting right on time, she hugged us again, smiled and then she was gone.

"See you, Thelma! Come back soon won't you?" Romana shouted.

CHAPTER TWELVE

It was a strange kind of limbo feeling we experienced for the next couple of weeks. Romana had the phone calls once a week to say all was going to plan. Albeit a coded message, it was a brief conversation. But this gave her some reassurance, given she didn't want to have any part in this escapade, especially as it was so far away in Europe.

I promised her once this was sorted we would go to London so she could see for herself where I came from. Mind you, I wouldn't remember too much about London. What with the war changing the face of London during the time I was away fighting and returning back there to now. Well I suppose the famous landmarks were still intact. So at least we could do those sights. The exhibition date at the Tate was the day after tomorrow, a Friday. It would run for three weeks. So by all accounts Scott and the FBI team should have made the switch on the ferry by now. It was the Wednesday before the opening. For all of Wednesday Romana and I kept asking each other: "Do you think they have done it?"

We had no way of knowing until the evening of the Thursday when our doubts and questions were answered by the phone call from Brenda. She said how she and her brother were now able to confirm their vacation date to come and stay here at the Ocean's Pantry. After a lot of hassle at work her brother was able to finally get time off to travel. She booked two rooms for a week arriving in just three weeks' time. This was like music to our ears. Romana was so happy.

For the first time in quite a few weeks she had that magical glow about her again.

Despite Rodrigo being told initially by Scott that he would be on his way to Australia after the job in London and consequently be away from here for some weeks, he would in fact travel with the cargo from Southampton directly to Colon, the busy port at the mouth of the Panama Canal. The load would be transferred to a smaller boat and come directly into our quayside here. This meant the artworks had been successfully switched on the ferry and by now should be at the dockside in Southampton, if not already loaded for the journey down to here in South America.

I wondered how long it would take before it was announced that the heist had occurred and in turn broadcast to the world. It would be broadcast for sure as this would support the fact that the shipment Rodrigo was wanting was in fact, the genuine thing, the real deal. Of course this news only meant that one part of this operation had been successful. In some ways the hardest and certainly the most dangerous as far as Scott was concerned was yet to happen. That would be here when the goods finally arrived and the all-important meeting would take place between Scott and Rodrigo.

The sea journey could be for anything up to nine days depending on the weather. We had no way of knowing what the conditions were, as our weather forecasting only covered our direct location. We might hear of something on the news if a hurricane was brewing up off Florida but that was it. So once again the waiting game continued. A few days before we anticipated Scott and the cargo's arrival, Rodrigo called in for a lunchtime drink. He had in tow the two guys we had seen at his brother's bar all those weeks ago. I wasn't there but Romana did say her heart sank to the pit of her stomach when she saw them head her way crossing the road from where Rodrigo always parked his car. But she held her own she said, knowing what was at stake and that she had to put on a brave face whatever was said to her during this impromptu visit.

As it happened the three men sat quietly chatting at a table at the front of the restaurant. Rodrigo made small talk with Romana as she took their order. Her heart was racing. She half expected being quizzed about Scott and his absence just now, but thankfully, no such questions were aimed at her. As quickly as they came, they went. Rodrigo's customary kissing of Romana's hand as if he were some kind of aristocratic gentleman in front of his uncouth associates.

The next week came and went with our expectations of a reunion with Scott growing each day. Likewise, we spoke about when, and if, Thelma and Jerry would arrive back with us. But then again, would they show up here, just in case it raised any suspicion? Based on our 'need to know' basis we speculated on so many permutations as to what might occur. Then of course, Brenda and her brother might in fact be replacements for Thelma and Jerry. All would be revealed in the fullness of time, which was for sure.

Unexpectedly Brenda phoned Romana to tell her she would be at the Ocean's Pantry tomorrow evening at around seven o'clock in the evening. All of a sudden the weeks that had passed had all palled into the distant past. Romana made sure her daily shop at the quayside was to bring in some top quality fare for what was hopefully to be a celebration meal with Scott's home coming.

There was a great sigh of relief that the waiting game was drawing to a close. We are very structured us humans. We need routine; we need to know what is happening. It is fair to say even the most laid back of mankind needs to know. He needs to know when his next meal is coming, needs to know what the weather is going to be. Often he needs to know the most trivial of things, but it always hinges around him knowing. Mankind doesn't like uncertainty. We were coming out of that uncertain period but moving into a more serious time. What had happened in Europe was an age away, although we knew a little about the bigger game plan.

From now on we would be involved to a degree in the game rather than just sitting on the sidelines. But we also knew we had to step up to the plate and play our part when required to engineer the comeuppance of Rodrigo.

I couldn't but help notice a couple of new faces hanging around the quayside this morning as I pulled my jeep around to the back of the Ocean's Pantry. One did toss his head upwards in a sort of 'hello' type gesture. I can't say I had ever seen him before. Hopefully, I thought, was he was an undercover FBI chap? He must have been, I tried to reassure myself. My suspicions were answered when Romana greeted me with a peck on the cheek. She informed me we had two new guests staying for a week.

"We have two gentlemen who have come to Los Santos for the fishing." They were booked into rooms three and six. Both were from New York, although one did seem to have less of a New York accent than the other.

Seven o'clock saw our two new guests leaning against the bar having a beer. I introduced myself to them as Enrico poured me a beer.

"Yes we know who you are," the chap on my right said. He was the New Yorker with his unmistakable city drawl. "I'm Conrad and this is Frank. We work together in downtown Manhattan. Insurance don't you know. We're just down here for about a week or so, doin' some fishing."

"Yeah, we hope to bag a big one, if you get what I mean?" Frank said. His accent was definitely not New York. He was from the south, Carolina he went on to tell me when I asked. We of course had the obligatory banter about Yanks and Limeys. There is no bar on the planet given this situation wouldn't be complete without this conversation taking place.

The light-hearted atmosphere changed when a car, a taxi, pulled up directly outside of the restaurant. Their actions cemented my suspicions, they were with the FBI. They stood up straighter, their eyes moving quickly in all directions from the car in the centre of their vision to the side tables of the restaurant and beyond.

No need for alarm though, as I had thought it was going to be Scott getting out of the taxi. Due to the tides he had docked along the coast and got a cab rather than wait for the higher tide to get into our harbour.

"He's here, Romana!" I shouted. Both of them ran into one another's arms.

"Good to be home I'd say," Conrad said.

"Sure thing, bet I don't that get kinda welcome when I go home next week," Frank remarked.

After a couple of drinks it was decided all of us would eat together. As the meal progressed the talk became more serious. It was apparent to all, we all of us knew who the others were so to speak. Frank made the first play.

"You say you've been away, Scott? Europe I heard?"

Scott looked a little sheepish given what Jerry and Thelma had told him not to trust anyone.

"I said I'd been away but I didn't say where," Scott replied.

"Scott, I know you have. I know you were in Paris two weeks ago on Tuesday."

"Hell I know you were," Conrad chipped in. "I sold you a newspaper as you came out of your apartment on Rue de la Avignon each morning. I've had a shave since then and changed my sunglasses. No point kidding anymore, we need to work together. Jerry and Thelma will be here tomorrow night. They will explain all and what happens next. I know you have been through it with them a million times, Scott, but view it as a sort of refresher. We want Rodrigo, and badly at that."

Frank turned to Romana. "Thelma spoke to me about your concerns when Scott was away. Well now he is back we just want you to know he is being looked out for more than you can imagine. Scott has got close to Rodrigo. Closer than anyone else before, and as Conrad said, we want him put away so he can't keep exploiting people here in his little empire. But more importantly he can't keep supplying the crap he does to the States and even Europe, if you know what I mean."

Scott was quite quiet but given the circumstances it was plain to see both he and Romana wanted to be alone and just talk I guess. This in mind I decided to allow them to do just that. So once we had all eaten I offered to help clear up before my two new friends and I would sample the best drinking spots of town starting at the by now infamous Mermaid's Resting Place bar. I wondered what kind of reception would be given to me this time round with two new faces to the town.

I explained to Frank and Conrad about Mario, Philippe's brother as we walked through town to the Mermaid. Conrad assured me that they had been well briefed about Mario. I was to say that they were staying at the Ocean's Pantry, which they were. And that they were hoping to get some serious fishing done which was the main purpose of their trip. As was to be expected we got the mandatory silence as we entered the bar. Mario as usual was cleaning a glass with a tea towel which could have done with a clean itself. He put down the glass and nodded in my direction.

"Good evening, Joe. What can I get you?"

"Oh three beers please, Mario. Don't let me stop the rest of your friends from having fun. Please put some music on, it seems awfully quiet in here tonight. I was rather hoping to show this place off as I know it can be. Full of local charm and spirit."

Mario nodded again this time in the direction of a man who was leaning against the juke box. He flicked the power switch on the wall and the music kicked into life. "Three beers, you want anything to chase with 'em?" Mario asked.

"Now you're talking," Frank interjected.

"Frank Williamson." He held out his hand to Mario who in turn limply shook Frank's.

"My buddy Conrad and me are here staying at the Ocean's Pantry for a week. We've come down here to do some serious fishing. Joe thought it a good idea to go somewhere after dinner for a serious drink. So what ya say we have a good drink?"

I went on to tell Mario how Romana was hoping to attract more people to the Pantry to make use of the rooms above the restaurant. Her aim was to encourage fishermen. Tying in with the local boats would help their livelihoods and then she could cook the day's catch in a way only she could, as we all knew so well. The story had seemed to have been believed by all and soon one by one the other customer's came and chatted. I suppose that over time the locals had no trust or confidence in anyone who was not known to them. This was born out of the corrupt and deceitful regime that had haunted them for years. That regime was under the rule of one Philippe Rodrigo. Well, all things being equal, the time was due to turn on the fortunes of Rodrigo's empire.

The evening passed without any incident. The only conversation was small talk. In the main it was about fishing, of which both Frank and Conrad had a good knowledge and quite passionate about the subject. They genuinely liked their fishing. It turned out, Frank told me on our walk home, their job takes them all around the world and besides their standard issue Smith and Weston's they always both pack their fishing tackle.

"So either way when we say we're going fishing, we really are!" he quipped.

CHAPTER THIRTEEN

Still not knowing what was happening behind the scenes we kept ourselves busy. Frank and Conrad kept up their premise of being two guys on a fishing trip and they really were having a ball. The daily catches were something to behold to the other tourists on the quayside when they came back in from a morning's fish. They also had started to make friends with the fishermen, which was helping to secure their cover as just tourists themselves.

It was on the fifth night at dinner that Scott announced, "It's on for tomorrow. All systems go." He assured Romana additional agents were now in the area ready to move in on Rodrigo. He was to meet Philippe in the morning at the plantation house, ten thirty sharp. The cargo had been unloaded and was ready to be taken from a quayside warehouse to the house by truck for Rodrigo to see the merchandise. Scott would be accompanied by one of his cohorts from the heist in London. All of which Rodrigo knew about, this had been told to him prior to Scott going to Europe so there would be no surprises for Philippe to worry about. Needless to say Rodrigo was not in the know when it came to the FBI shadowing Scott and now basically crawling about in the plantations undergrowth waiting for the handover to happen. Dinner was at this point somewhat subdued for obvious reasons. Frank, who had over the last few days shown a real side of concern to his character, reassured Romana all would work out well. Likewise Thelma, who until this evening had been a little distant to us, was doing what she could to assure

Romana it was a matter of hours now not days or weeks as it had been previously.

"You just have to be strong for a little while longer. Then before you know it, this place will be back to how it should be. There'll be people coming here to have a good time. People living here having a good time too, knowing they are free of Rodrigo and his scams that they had to buy into like protection money. But protection from what, just him? Oh we want this man real bad, Romana. He's hurt a lot of people. Yes he has hurt wealthy people's pockets by stealing their invaluable art collections. But you know what? Once their insurance company has paid out they will have forgotten all about whatever it was that he had taken from them. Those that didn't have insurance, well they hurt a bit more. But they usually have so much money they just fill the gap on the wall left by the theft with somethin' else. They soon forget and move on. No it ain't those people we necessarily want to help. It's the Romana's, Scott's and even Mario's of this world. Take Manuel down there on the quayside fixing his nets. He needs new nets but he can't afford them because what little profit he makes from his day's catch he has to pay to one of Rodrigo's henchmen as protection money. That's how they make their money up. Oh yes, Rodrigo he don't even pay his nearest and dearest the going rate. He just sucks them in to believing that one day they will get the 'big' bonus. Thing is, they're all gullible to believe him. It's fair to say the only bonus has been going into Rodrigo's pocket not that of his workforce."

By ten dinner was over, a final night cap by ten thirty and we went our separate ways to bed. I quietly had a word with Romana, telling her all that Thelma had said. All would be good sooner than you can say 'Bob's your uncle' or 'Dad' as we often joked. I gave her a final glance over my shoulder as I got into the jeep for the journey back to mine.

The black clear sky spread out in front of me as I got to the crest of the headland, stopping momentarily I again looked back to the town. No real thoughts came into my head. My mind had been so busy of late working out all the scenarios I had thought could happen about tomorrow's, hopefully, final meeting between Scott and Rodrigo, I resigned myself to think Scott was in good hands and by this time tomorrow we would all be celebrating. I sat myself straight in the seat, I was just glad to drive back home and rest my mind.

The dawn chorus woke me. There is no alarm clock quite like the screech of gulls and parrots competing for their share of the sky. Not unlike Rodrigo, I thought. He has everything going for him and has had for years, but he still wants more. Those birds have the entire sky to fly around and they still want someone else's space. Crazy!

Although still dark I got up and put the coffee on. Today was not a day to lay in bed despite the fact that it took me ages to get off to sleep the night before. Showered, shaved and dressed I watched the sun rise from my balcony. This was beginning to be a bit of a regular habit, this getting up early. So, I thought, 'act normal'. But that's easier said than done. The coffee was welcome but I certainly didn't feel like breakfast. I cleaned through, a bit to occupy my time, but I can't say my mind was really focused on the chores I was doing. I would persist until ten o'clock then drive to town.

Hoovered, dusted, also the kitchen and bathroom cleaned, it was still only nine thirty-five. There's only one thing for it, let's have another coffee. At this rate I would never be able to get off to sleep again tonight having had all this caffeine. I sat on the veranda and watched the surfers catching the waves, even after all these years it still mesmerized me in some kind of hypnotic and relaxing way. There were one or two couples walking hand in hand along the shoreline, all of them blindly in love, without a care in the world. Hopefully in a day or two it would be Scott and Romana doing the self-same thing. Glancing between my watch and the surfers it seemed every minute ticked by at a slow and lethargic pace.

I closed the door to the bungalow in what can only be described as a trance and jumped into the jeep. It was the air of uncertainty that left me with this weird feeling. Not knowing how the day would pan out. I only just got to the headland seeing the town and harbour stretched out before me that I noticed a truck pass me going towards the plantation. It was only as the dust settled that it occurred to me it was Scott riding 'shotgun' with his partner in crime, so to speak, at the wheel. Oh well, this was it. Phase two and hopefully the final phase was in motion. Getting to the end of the pine-clad stretch, another truck came towards me. This one appeared to have several men in the back hidden slightly by the flapping canvas sides. Certainly they were either police or military.

I drove just another few hundred yards and two cars going at speed hurtled by. Jerry was in the driving seat of the first vehicle, he quickly raised his hand to say 'hello' and then he was gone. I can only think Thelma was either in that car with him or she would have definitely been in the following vehicle. Either way, the game was on. Deciding to take a minute, I pulled over to my right. The small pull-in offered a fabulous view of the bay with far-reaching views out to sea. Turning off the motor on the jeep I took in the whole vista. The gentle breeze whistled lightly through the pines trees above me. Contemplating what was about to happen at the Rodrigo estate in the next few minutes or so, I was left feeling as if I was in some kind of surreal limbo. How did this happen to me? How did I get embroiled in all of this? This was certainly heavy duty, especially with the FBI being involved. What would I be doing now if I'd stayed in England? So many questions, but irrespective of the assumed answers I was here, right or wrong. Thinking on, the events unfolding at Rodrigo's were being dealt with as I sat there mulling over my options. By all account, this time tomorrow he would be on American soil awaiting his destiny. Payback time for all his scheming and manipulative ways he had used over the years to gain all the wealth he had accumulated. I have been able to get close to Romana the daughter I thought I had lost forever because of my behaviour after her mother's passing. I was pretty confident soon I would gain a son-in-law who had shown great strength and commitment to Romana. It had been many years since I could say I had met with some 'good' friends who I am sure I could trust, rather than my usual bar room acquaintances. Yes, hopefully Thelma and Jerry would stay in touch between their worldwide exploits and adventures. Silly old fool, I thought. Why would you want to ever think of what life might have been like had you have stayed in grey, damp and cold England. Just look around you, breathe it in, smell it, listen. This is what life is all about. This is what life is meant to be like. Some people would give their right arm to live here. Live this adventure rather than sit in some claustrophobic Dickensian office, staring out of the window each day waiting for the weekend. Then when it does come the weather is wet and cold so you end up staring out of your house window waiting for, well nothing really, just waiting. But always dreaming, dreaming of this view, this way of life. I smiled and then laughed out loud. No one was about to hear my laughter, but even if they were they wouldn't have commented or gestured, if anything people would jus think 'it's that old fool who lives on his own in the beach bungalow'. So was the way of life here. Remember how Sam had said he just drove out to the headland some nights just to look at the stars? Just take it all in, enjoy it and I guess inwardly appreciate this little piece of heaven on earth.

Starting the motor again I pulled the brim of my hat down to shade me from the warming morning sun and headed down as I had a million times before towards the jewel in all of this, the Ocean's Pantry. Romana was serving breakfast to a couple off one of the yachts that had moored over night at the quayside. She nodded to me to go with her into the kitchen. Sensing she was perplexed I followed quickly.

"It's happening now!" she said through gritted teeth in a concerned tone. I reassured her all would be fine. Given the waiting she had endured recently, what was another couple of hours? I did my best to make light of the situation but also wanted to be there for her, supporting her at this time.

"Come on, let's get busy. How's the couple for coffee? Shall I top them up? Look, you know he is in good hands. The number of blokes I saw in the back of the truck and cars amounted to a small army in comparison to Rodrigo's manpower. Just a couple more hours that's all. Then all of this will be over. Now coffee, I'll serve the couple out front. Come on busy, busy."

Before we knew it another few tables had customers wanting breakfast. I asked one couple where they were moored up. Sometimes, although you get into the harbour, you might have to tie up on the east-side which means the only way to the quayside is by tender. But no, they were in fact staying at the hotel.

"So, not that we want to turn away custom, but why breakfast here?" I gingerly asked. "The hotel is fabulous. They have great rooms, great service and good food. But not great food, not fantastic personal service and certainly nothing of a view compared to here."

"Mind if I write that down and pin it to the front wall?" I replied laughing.

"Be my guest. This is what we want when we come away. Local friendly service, none of that mass manufactured processed national franchised kind of service you get in those big hotels. Oh sorry, I must introduce us, Daniel and Julie Woods." He stood up and offered his hand. I shook it returning the favour of introducing myself and Romana in her absence.

"Ever thought about leaving the manufactured processed national chain for your evening dinner? I believe there is a very good seafood restaurant not a million miles from where we are now." We all laughed and talked some more. Romana emerged once again from the kitchen; I beckoned her over and introduced her formally.

"Do I take it you would like one of our front row tables for two this evening then?" I again gingerly asked.

"You certainly can, Joe. Seven for seven thirty, just the two of us but don't be surprised if you get a few more customers come on down from the hotel."

"Oh the more the merrier it will be. We'll get you all in somehow! Any which way, we will look to seeing you tonight," I replied.

Glancing over my shoulder, Romana looked in my direction giving me a wry smile. Maybe just a little nervous given what was playing on our minds. But I remembered how Thelma had said we must make the effort and keep to our normal routine.

"Okay, young lady. You heard the man, we must get busy and prepare for tonight. I reckon it's going to be somewhat special here at the old Ocean's Pantry," I quipped at her, clapping my hands as we both walked back into the kitchen.

We got into our daily routine of preparing vegetables for the evening dinner. Romana popped down to the harbour as always to get the pick of the fish from the boys on the quay. We didn't talk much to one another as we went about our chores. Enrico too, he was noticeably quieter than usual. Although he wasn't party to what was happening just a couple of miles away out of town at Rodrigo's house, his sixth sense kicked in giving him a gut feeling that things were far from normal around the restaurant today.

Around four o'clock we sat down for a cool drink of home-made sparkling lemonade. Romana as usual had not just poured the drink into a glass for each of us, but had sliced thin wedges of lime which now stood vertically, dripping into the drink. The jagged ice cubes added to this simple refreshing interlude for the three of us. We had had a quiet lunch time with only five tables to serve. But just now the atmosphere was beginning to get quite tense with anticipation. Every car engine that was heard coming towards us from the direction of the headland road saw us all in unison looking with, no doubt, an expression of exasperation as just another car drove on by.

Then finally the relative peace of this balmy afternoon was interrupted by the blaring of a car horns. Away in the distance just now, but coming from the direction of the headland road across the bay. It was getting progressively louder by the second.

"That must be them!" I shouted with the excitement of a school kid. But Romana shouted over me saying there was more than one horn blasting, and sure enough listening closer another horn could be heard, and another. What was going on? Moments later they came into view. There were two cars and a truck bringing up the rear. Scott and Thelma were the first to jump out the leading car which had been driven by Jerry. Scott who had been sat in the back of Thelma and Jerry's car, harbourside as it were, leapt over the bonnet and vaulted over one of the front tables towards Romana.

"It's done! It's all sorted. He won't be seeing this beautiful place for a long time. He admitted everything." Jerry by now was with us.

"He's right, he coughed up to everything, and I mean

everything, Joe," Jerry went on to say. "Turns out he was a main contact here after the war for the Nazis. He was paying some of the fishermen to pick up Germans from the islands further up the coast. At that time there was a small airstrip on one of the islands which is now all but overgrown. Argentina's President Peron opened up the borders and the country to the ex-Nazis using the ratlines via the Vatican in Rome. This was after he pledged more or less his allegiance to the Catholic Church having become a member of the Catholic Church. The majority of them came in by ship via Buenos Airies. Our intelligence, aided by Jewish Holocaust survivors who have been trying to locate and bring their captors to justice over the years, have been able to piece together the intricate puzzle surrounding the disappearance of what would seem to be thousands of Nazis. And yes, I mean thousands. Anything up to seven or eight thousand Nazis are said to have made their way here into South America. It would appear that the Italians did figure highly in the war effort after all, albeit after the event. You see Peron, being made a man of the church, gained support from the Italians and more importantly for him the Vatican. He got the title of Argentina Delegation of Immigration in Europe, whose headquarters were in Rome. A priest by the name of Jose Clemente Silva is the brother of one of Peron's closest friends, Oscar Silva. Now he was an absolute ultra nationalist in Peron's regime. The priest was sent to Rome with the sole intention of getting somewhere in the region of four million Europeans into Argentina. They wanted doctors, nurses, scientists, engineers – you name it they wanted it. It was as if Peron wanted to build his own super race.

"Scott's right, he won't be back here for a long, long time – not with what we have now. In all my years doing this I have never seen a man roll over like he did. It was as if he knew his time of high life through ill-gotten gains was up."

"Wow! I can't believe Rodrigo was so, well, 'big'. I just had him down for a small time big fish in a small pond kind of bully boy really. Not into all this heavy duty stuff. Anyway, I knew it would work out for the better. But where is he now?" I asked.

"Oh he and his henchmen are safely locked up on their way to Florida as we speak," Thelma said. "We got there a bit before ten, but you know that, Joe, cos you saw us just this side of your place, didn't you?" Thelma started to tell us. "Well anyway, we parked up the vehicles about a quarter of a mile back from the house and got the guys to spread out around the plantation basically surrounding the place. Me and Jerry took cover in the truck which Scott was driving. Along side him in the cab was Alberto. A man of few words, he had been shoulder to shoulder with Scott from the minute he had landed in Europe. We donned our listening headsets, then just as planned, Scott and Alberto here–" I gestured a hello nod in Alberto's direction. Thelma continued, "They just knocked the door, Rodrigo came out with one of his henchmen in tow to the back of the truck and he was shown some of the work. Rodrigo then summoned a few more guys from the side of the house to help unload the rest of the pieces. That was fun, you see me and Jerry were holding on for dear life to the suspension whilst all this was going on. When Rodrigo said about unloading the truck in the big barn, I don't know about you, but I thought it's one thing holding on for your dear life while this thing is parked up, but it's another when the damn thing is moving. My god it was bumpy from the main road down his drive to the house." We all laughed.

Jerry cut in, "Anyway, with the works all unloaded in the main entrance hall of the house another face appeared on the scene. Daniel Coignet, a French man who we have heard about in the past. There have always been rumours about this guy and shall we say his 'business dealings' in the European art world. So Thelma and me are listening in to the conversation that's taking place and sure enough Coignet is doing his thing, gotta hand it to the man he knows his stuff. He picked up a lot, and I mean a lot, of fine detail. He made comments on just about every piece in that haul. You gotta give it to him. So he verifies to Rodrigo that the boys here had brought the goods. The real deal, as it were. And that's when Scott had to do his bit for the final sting. Work of art in itself I'd say."

"How were you feeling at this point then, Scott?" Romana asked.

"I was absolutely petrified. It was a case of keeping cool and going through the routine we had rehearsed I don't know how many times, heh Jerry?" Scott looked towards Jerry, who by now was smirking like a Cheshire cat who had got the cream.

"I started by saying, 'you know what, Philippe, I've now done my side of the deal and proved my worth, it's your turn now'. God did I swallow hard after saying that! My throat was so dry and Rodrigo knew this. He got one of his guys to get me some water. But in doing so he was just standing there staring at me. I thought I had blown it, but then remembered what Jerry had told me. It would be like this, be honest, and tell him straight. So I did, I had never been this close to making a deal like this which would give me the big break I needed. Sure enough Rodrigo's harsh gaze abated and he complimented me on my honesty, rather ironic really. Then he passed me the water from the tray that had now arrived. I swallowed down a huge gulp, looked up to see four guys pull in a small cart-like trolley from that side room to the left of his staircase. That room looked as if it went along the length of that side of the house cos I caught a glimpse of a window at the far end of the room. The view was down towards the south side of the plantation. Anyway his gorilla by now had un-wrapped a couple of the packages. Sure enough they were full of white powder, could have been sherbet for all I knew but that is where Alberto comes in. Alberto is our 'Coignet'. The stuff was one hundred per cent pure. I asked him if we had a deal, all of the 'Powder', for all of the 'Paint'. The whole delivery that Alberto and I had taken there today.

"After a couple minutes of Rodrigo having a quiet word with Coignet, which I have to say seemed like forever, a couple of nods and mutterings later and we had the deal sealed. I shook his hand and at the same time gave Thelma and Jerry the 'word' as it were. 'We're gonna be celebrating tonight, Alberto', and by the time I turned around to look at Alberto, Thelma and Jerry were inside the front door with about seven or eight other guys coming into the house from all ways. I gotta ask, Jerry, how did those two guys get not only into the house, but upstairs? When they came down it took everyone by surprise."

"Oh let's just say that is 'classified'."

Thelma carried on explaining, but as she did I couldn't help but notice how Romana was clinging on tight to Scott all this time. He ain't going anywhere was kind of written all over her face, I thought to myself. I tuned back into what Thelma was saying.

"We asked Philippe if he knew why we were there. And he just said it had only been a matter of time before he would be caught out. That said though, now at his age he had enjoyed the fruits of his spoils. He went on to say how he was just rattling round this old house on his own.

"Jerry suggested we went somewhere a little comfier to discuss this further. He agreed and we went through to his drawing room. Meanwhile our guys rounded up his men and of course Coignet. Oh I hope our guys didn't tighten the cuffs too much on you and Alberto?" Thelma said gesturing towards Scott and Alberto. They both shook their heads and smiled.

"Sorry about that, guys, but we had to make it look the real deal. Even now Rodrigo needs to think you are locked up, being investigated for us to really close the case. Anyway, Jerry and I sat down with him and he just started talking. 'Let me start way back, I have a lot to tell you guys. It was 1941 when I first met...'. I think those were his actual words at that time. After that we recorded all that was said."

Enrico, who I hadn't notice disappear in all the melee, weaved his way between the tables with a large tray of ice cold beer bottles held aloft with much dexterity. It all seemed somewhat of a blur to me. Nazis, Peron, intelligence authorities – you name it, it was in there.

I momentarily sat back, took a swig of my beer and looked around at what seemed like a sea of faces in front of me. There was much laughing and an air of relief that all the hard work that had gone into the operation by Jerry and Thelma's 'team' had been a great success. A lot of the guys in front of me I was seeing for the first time, but it felt as though I knew each and every one of them somehow. It was at this point I thought something, or at least someone, was missing, and there as if by telepathy, Sam was standing just outside of the restaurant terrace. Moving out to see him I felt a broad smirk come across my face. "It's over, Sam; they've got him lock, stock and barrel. He's admitted everything; he won't be going anywhere now other than Florida, but it won't be for a vacation."

We walked across the road and sat on a bench overlooking the harbour. I repeated to Sam what had been said by the others when they got back to the restaurant. "How did you know to come here just now anyway?" I asked him.

"Believe it or not I heard the horns blaring as they came

over the headland road into town. I'm surprised the whole town wasn't here to see what was happening cos they must 'ave heard it!" We both laughed, not by way of his quip but also with an air of relief. After many years of frustration we knew that Rodrigo's wealth and power, which had been grown out of the hardship and bullying of others, was now at an end.

"Let's take a walk, Joe. Let's go back to the old dockside office. I got a bottle of rum here. I think we should toast those who are not here to enjoy this moment. Let's go down there where it all started and we can finally put it to rest – the torture that man caused us. Whatta you say, old friend?"

"I say, I'll get another bottle from the bar and we will make it a double celebration!"

With our arms over each other's shoulders we strolled back across to the Ocean's Pantry laughing out loud as we went. Romana broke away from Scott. "You two seem happy. I know I have told you off before for it, but I guess this time you have every right to celebrate. But please, not too much!"

"Were you listening in on our conversation over there?" I said pointing back to the bench we had been sitting on.

"No, why do you say that? Of course not, but it would be good to have Jerry and Thelma's bugging device sometimes to find out what you two have planned. No, I know that you, more than anyone, will want to have a drink to bid Rodrigo good riddance. Go, go have fun but as I said, not too much, heh?"

Like a couple of young teenagers just about to do some kind of dare or get up to what they know is mischief, we grinned at each other and set off towards the old dockside buildings.

Although the sun was still high and warm there was a slightly subdued atmosphere between us the closer we got. Walking silently as we got to what was a thriving hive of activity some twenty or thirty years ago we looked up and around the old tired derelict buildings. Windows were smashed either by kids or just by the passing of stormy weather that sometimes batters this part of the world on occasion. The names of the companies that owned and ran these warehouses were faded and in some cases unrecognizable. Some of the largest trading companies in Europe had storage facilities here where cargo would be brought on large ocean going ships. The loads from each large ship was broken down here and transferred on to smaller vessels that in turn would steam up and down this coast to the smaller ports for distribution. But with the advent of air cargo, these loads could be flown directly to these places. One by one the companies closed their warehouses along the quayside, doing away with the labour of many men needed to work here.

Grass grew up between the cracks in the once hard surface of concrete which was the roadway for trucks that had thundered up and down between these huge sheds. That hardness had gone, that harsh masculine environment that was once all that this area ever represented. All of that had disappeared apart from the fact that the buildings, albeit a shadow of their former selves, remained, but now with an almost softened atmosphere about them. There was an air of tranquillity that now blew gently up between the largest grain stores this side of the US and a warehouse that was nicknamed the Trading Post. That had just about every conceivable thing you could think of go through its huge hangar-like loading bay doors. I remember seeing crates with boat and truck parts. Drink, whiskey and bourbon, cigarettes by the truck load. All heading for every town and village the length and breadth of this beautiful country I now called my home.

Sam and I found ourselves at the bottom of the stairway

that Bob and I had found Juanita. I momentarily closed my eyes. I could visualise her lying there on that fateful day many years previously. I felt Sam place his hand on my shoulder and squeeze down in a sort of reassuring kind of way.

Standing motionless and staring for a minute I gathered my thoughts and visualized again the scene.

"Just think," Sam said cutting the silence. "You have Romana now who keeps Juanita's memory alive. Come on; let's get one of these bottles opened."

We walked around to the water's edge side of the building and sat down on one of the many capstans that fringed the quay. Twisting the cap off of the rum I flicked it into the water.

"Well, you know what that means? We'll have to finish this."

"I can't see that being a problem," Sam said. A broad smile spread across his face. Taking a slug from the bottle I passed it to him. Again we said nothing, just smiled to one another. For the first time in a long time there was an air of contentment. Ten or fifteen minutes passed with neither of us saying a word. We surveyed the old quayside and all of its buildings, thinking of the people who worked here and the stories. The creaking old buildings spoke back to us, with the odd grinding sound of rusty hinges scraping against the door frame as it swings somewhere inside with the gentle afternoon breeze moving it to and fro. Birds, mainly some kind of pigeon, flapped out from the rafters occasionally, no doubt off to seek some food before the sun sets on them another day.

I glanced at Sam. He had his chin cupped in his right hand, running his thumb up and down his cheek. There was a definite expression of thought on his face. He was obviously contemplating something. As I thought, he turned to me now folding his arms, still sitting on the capstan.

"You know what, Joe? You think the last few weeks and months have been stressful? Well I bet that ain't nothing on what's going to happen to you next!"

I turned to face him, only to see the broadest of smiles returning to his friendly face.

"And what do you mean by that?" I asked.

"Joe, you are going to be dragged into 'wedding' arrangements! You wait and see!" He laughed out loud.

"No not yet. Admittedly I kinda guess Romana and young Scott will get together but not for a while. Don't you think?"

Laughing, Sam said, "Got you thinking now, old man!" We both laughed. Exchanging a few more quips on the subject and still laughing even louder, by now both of us were almost crying. A mixture of happiness and of course relief all rolled into one. All of our emotions were being vented, like some huge pressure valve inside us had just been opened. It wasn't just the recent events of the 'sting', but everything that had led up to it.

"You know what, Joe? I know one thing is a dead cert. You won't be in charge of the bar!"

Our bellows were cut short when we heard our names being called. It was Romana and Scott.

"Heh, Joe! Where are you?"

"What did I say, Joe?" Sam smirked. "Maybe you're gonna find out the wedding date sooner than you thought!" He laughed again.

"I reckon you might be right, old man. Oh my bloody god!" I said with an almost sobering shiver running through me.

"How much have you two had to drink?" Romana scalded.

"If you have come to tell me what I think you are going to tell me, probably not enough!"

Sam couldn't contain himself anymore and just burst with laughter, me too.

Romana now joined by Scott stood hand in hand in front of me, beaming.

"Uncle Joe, I mean Dad. Scott has asked me to..." I chipped in quicker than a flash and finished her sentence. "...Marry him!" I blurted.

"Well er, yes. You're not surprised, you don't mind?"

"Me surprised? No not me. I had it on the cards for a long time," I cheekily said glancing over my shoulder to Sam.

"I couldn't be happier for the both of you. Sam and I were just saying how so proud I have been of you. Not just today but ever since you were small and growing up. All the things you have done, what with the Ocean's Pantry and all. Wasn't that right, Sam? What we were just saying?" Sam came forward with open arms towards the two of them.

"Congratulations! I just know you are going to be so very happy together."

"This calls for a celebration! Come on, let's get back to the Pantry and un-cork some vintage champagne!" I quickly interjected.

Arms linked, Scott and Romana walked with me and Sam on either side of them with our arms draped on their shoulders. We headed back to the restaurant where there was a long overdue party about to be had.

Jerry and Thelma stood on the pavement in front of the canopy, both smiling.

"Heh Joe, you'll have to brush off your best bib and tucker now and get that speech sorted." I hugged Thelma and shook Jerry's hand.

"Romana, oh my god, when? You haven't told me when. Thelma's right, I will need to get my suit cleaned and, and! Oh my god, when?" I suddenly blurted. Linking her arm in mine tightly and pointing her left index finger on my nose, Romana cut across me.

"Don't worry, at least twelve months. Scott will be going

with Jerry and Thelma to Miami to sit the court case of Rodrigo. In any case there is no way you are going to wear to my wedding that old suit of yours anyway, whether you get it cleaned or not! No. Like it or not, you and I will be going shopping, and not here but in Miami!" Everyone roared with laughter.

"I tell you what, that Rodrigo has a lot to answer for, believe you and me!" I shouted.

Needless to say we all had one hell of a night. Too much to drink yes, but the sunrise as ever was outstanding. Well what I could see of it through a really heavy hangover.

CHAPTER FOURTEEN

The next few months were spent with all of us going about our daily chores much as usual. Given the potential severity and implications of the case, there was representation from numerous countries from across Europe as well as the USA. Despite the speed about which the case came about, it was as if a lot of these officials were on standby for such an event. Maybe they were? On standby that is. Maybe there were others out there who were being sought and the authorities just needed that break to bring them to justice, just as it had happened down our way.

The court case in Miami saw Scott flitting between here in the bay and the mainland. It seemed an age some weeks when he was away for three or four nights on the trot. But on reflection the time had flown by. Rodrigo didn't contested anything. It was as if he wanted to unburden his wrong doings of some many years. Charges brought against him and some of his heavies meant none of them would be out for many, many years. The case lasted some eight weeks. There were a couple of occasions when additional evidence needed to be gathered as requested by the defending lawyer and the judge. Although this threw up an air of disappointment because of further delays, the evidence was soon delivered to the court by the prosecuting team. It would appear that Jerry and Thelma, along with their team, had done a thorough job of getting every last shred of evidence to pin on Rodrigo. I remembered one day how Thelma had told me they wanted this guy so bad and how they had come so very close on a few times before. But Rodrigo had always just been that one step in front of them. It was only with our involvement, or in particular Scott's, that justice could be brought against him.

What came out in court made worldwide news. It turned out that Rodrigo had had connections with some of Europe's leading art dealers prior to the war. As the Nazi Third Reich grew in power across occupied Europe stealing art as it went, Rodrigo was the link between the Nazis and South America. It was always suspected but never confirmed, that he was also the link to Peron.

It was suggested various artwork came to be in his possession during the war years, more than likely via Rodrigo and his German connections. The plan being that after world domination Hitler, a keen collector of art, would have a collection by far and away greater than anyone pretty much on the planet, let alone in the Western world. The idea was for the majority of the Nazi Third Reich to have headquarters in Germany, but also here in South America. Peron's involvement with the Nazis also came to light as evidence files from another case, which had not quite been proved for certain but Rodrigo confirmed the fact, that Peron had during the war sold some ten thousand blank Argentine passports to the 'organisation of former SS members', known as ODESSA.

The organisation was set up during 1944 by some of the leading SS men, industrialists and even bankers in the event of defeat. Rodrigo not only confirmed this, but also probably more importantly for the German prosecutors, the whereabouts of some of the Nazi's leading figures. Because the court was a closed affair to both the press and the public, a number of leading officials from the Nazi party were tracked down and arrested without the slightest hint of knowing the authorities would be knocking on their door in the early hours, all due to Rodrigo's whistle blowing.

Further cases came to court over the coming months which also led to world headlines. Some of the atrocities that came out in the courts brought mass abomination for the Nazi regime of those dark days. In some ways it was a closure for a lot of people regarding exactly what went on in those camps. But of course there was for others, the re-opening of deep wounds left by their captors. I suppose justice will always be like that.

All through of the court case, Romana had been working behind the scenes on her wedding preparations. She had also flown to Miami and met with Thelma. The two of them had become quite close. Thelma had been able to arrange flights to coincide with Scott's court room appointments.

Meanwhile, Sam and I would spend a quiet evening once a week playing cards at the Mermaid's Resting Place. It was quite refreshing, the change in reception Sam and I had the first time we went there during Rodrigo's hearing. We knew it was a gamble as to how Mario, Rodrigo's younger brother, would greet us. But it was as if we had had been long lost friends. Not just Mario, but also the other guys who frequented the bar. In fact the bar itself transformed in the weeks that followed from a seedy, shadowy back street bar into a quaint, just off the tourist trail 'locals' bar which would welcome anyone wanting to come in and share or hear a good story. Sam and I even picked up a bit of work from Mario. I helped out doing some long overdue maintenance and redecorating around the place and Sam did the odd shift now and again to give Mario a night off.

Redecoration was also at the top of Romana's list of things to be done ready for the wedding. The six guest rooms were completely repainted and some of the furniture was re-placed. I suppose it is only fair that a paying guest should not have to put their foot up against the wall in order to gain leverage when opening a dressing table drawer.

Downstairs was also refreshed. New brightly coloured canopies replaced the somewhat sun-bleached ones of old that had seen, to be honest, better days. We also tiled the small wall and pavement to match, making it easier to wash down and keep clean. Before, it had always been a rather dusty uneven walkway.

There was a period of some three weeks when I didn't go home to my beach house as I would be starting at around six thirty in the morning and working through until maybe nine or ten at night. I was only stopping for a snack and soft drink. Yes, believe it or not I went teetotal during this time. But thankfully I wasn't on my own as Romana had employed a couple of local guys who had previously worked out at the Kumota Plaza. They had come into the Ocean's Pantry one night for a meal with their wives. We got talking and before we knew it they had agreed to come and work for Romana. They had been thinking of going out on their own anyway as they felt they could make a go of being their own boss. In any case many people had asked them to do some work around their houses. But because of the hours they kept out at the hotel they just couldn't. This was the break they needed.

We had a good time and our working relationship grew. Local customers coming into the Pantry would ask who did our work and we would gladly recommend the boys, Manuel and Roberto.

Like so much in people's lives, time marches by at an ever increasing pace the older one gets. I was no exception. It was as if it was only yesterday when I arrived in this beautiful part of the world and only yesterday that I met with some of the warmest friendliest people in the world, and this was still the case today. I had a family now, albeit all grown up, but I was sure in the not too distant future there would be more than one addition.

CHAPTER FIFTEEN

Saturday 21st June arrived, more or less twelve months after that day when Rodrigo was caught, once and for all. Now the day had arrived that would mark the start of this new life for us all down here.

The sky was a vivid blue, crystal clear, the breeze was light. Today I would walk my daughter down the aisle of the chapel which I had only visited once before. On that occasion it was her christening. A christening I didn't really embrace for fear of not being able to live up to her expectations. Back then I didn't really know of the importance of caring for someone other than myself. But I know now.

Life can be quite fraught at times and deal all of us an unlucky hand. But now, now for me life had come up trumps, a royal flush, and a full house all in one.

What can I say? Romana glowed. The service, simple but poignant expressed the love between her and Scott. The chapel was awash with colourful flowers, all of which we see in the hedgerows or fields around here and usually just pass by. But here today they showed off their real softness and beauty. Tied to each pew end they formed a colourful passage to the altar, where a magnificent display erupted with shades of pinks and soft blue.

It seemed the whole town had come out to celebrate as we paraded back to the Ocean's Pantry. People lined the street from the small chapel at the far end of the square around to the quayside where the restaurant stood all bedecked in flowers that matched Romana's bouquet and delicate head-dress. There was an atmosphere of sheer happiness in the air. Delight that now, finally after so many years, the whole regime that in these parts was Rodrigo's had been lifted. The slate wiped clean. People didn't just wave and smile as had been the case on the few wedding processions in town before. They cheered and whistled as if by way of relief.

Jerry and Thelma came for that weekend bringing with them a couple of colleagues who we had got to know over that troubled time. But today that was all behind us. It was as if today was the start of a new life for us all.

Thelma walked with me arm in arm behind Romana and Scott.

"You know what, Joe? I might need a room for a while. I gotta finish cataloguing all of Rodrigo's ill-gotten gains. You know anywhere that's just outside town, you know a bit quieter than the hustle bustle of a metropolis such as this? Something close to the beach, got a terrace where you can lie back in a hammock, grab a beer from the fridge and read a good book? You know of anywhere like that?" She smiled.

"Oh, I don't right now, but heh, I'll think of something, and when I do you'll be the first to know. Meanwhile, young lady, let's have a drink, a dance and some fun!"

It was a few weeks later whilst I was just having a quiet drink with Sam in the Mermaid's Resting Place, we were sitting, just looking, observing, people watching as usual. I noticed a man heading my way; he looks almost lost, I thought. Not lost in the sense of not knowing where he is, but lost in the sense of not fitting in.

"Mind if I join you?"

I nod, gesturing toward a chair for him. Sitting down directly opposite me he smiles albeit cautiously. I could feel myself frowning with a questionable expression on my face but not looking away from his almost penetrating deep blue eyes. Sam adjusted his posture sitting up straighter as if getting ready to leave.

The young man slowly put his beer down and reached into his inside jacket pocket. I was conscious of holding my stare looking directly into his eyes and he returning the same. I've found myself in many a poker game where each player has had to hold their nerve trying not to show the slightest hint of emotion.

"Anyone here look familiar?" he asked and placed an old faded and crumpled photograph on the table. Still holding my stare I reached down and picked up the piece of paper. Like being in a 'bubble' the music that was playing had now gone from my ears, my line of vision totally focused on the picture.

It was of a young man dressed in a British Army uniform. He had his arm around the shoulder of a brightly smiling young woman. Both were looking intently and happily at each other. She was pregnant.

"As I was saying," the young man repeated. "Anyone here look familiar?" His accent was English, with a definite southeast of the country twang. Sam broke the silence.

"You okay with this, Joe?"

"I think I have it, Sam. Why don't you give us a minute?"

Sam rose slowly, fixing a stare on our new visitor. "I'll be at the bar," Sam said quietly

I nodded but kept my gaze fixed on the youngster.

He drew another picture and another from his pocket.

"Here, you just as well have them all."

There was a slight air of aggression in his voice. Looking through the photographs I saw first a baby then progressively a small boy, a toddler, a teenager and finally a young man. It was the same young man who was sat across the table from me, albeit it was probably taken a couple of years previously.

I looked up from the pictures, staring intently into his

eyes. "How did you know where to find me?" I waited for his reply for what seemed to be an eternity.

"Oh you could say news travels fast." He paused again and continued. "The art heist back in London," he said with a rising intonation in his voice. "It seems you are somewhat of a hero not just in these parts, but also in England. Quite a few old boys were glad to see some of those Nazis put away behind bars, or at least sent to trial." The angry tone remained in his voice and he continued to speak. "So why did you just up and go? That's all I have come here to find out."

The anger was still there but with a quiver in it. Glancing at the photographs again I started to reply. Before I could start he cut in abruptly.

"And don't say it was a long time ago, things were different. You are my dad and you know it. Why did you run out on me and my mum?"

Taking a fresh intake of breath I carefully placed the pictures on the table in front of me, spreading them out in a line.

"Well, I will say that because it was! This picture of your mum and me was taken the day before I went off to North Africa. August 1942. We didn't know when or if I would return. Fact is, the next time I saw her you were nearly five I think. I walked back down a street I didn't recognise, to a house that had someone else's shirts hung in the wardrobe. You had a new dad and a mum I no longer knew. Like so many others at that time we were strangers. We were so far apart that we would probably never meet again in any kind of mutual affection or even friendship. We talked and talked. There was no animosity between us. We agreed she would stay with your dad, Derek wasn't it?"

My new friend cut in. "Daniel. Daniel Worthington."

I continued. "Talking of names," I questioned. "I take it you took Daniel's surname, but what is your first name? Is that still the same, Christopher?" again I asked with distinct question in my voice. He nodded in acknowledgement. I flicked my glance between the pictures and his face. He on the other hand just sat still as a rock staring at me. The atmosphere seemed to be subsiding with the air of aggression sliding into the background of this smoke-filled room wafting out through the open window shutters. After a minute or two of silence Christopher sat back into his chair having been sat on the edge of it. His whole demeanour was relaxed as if a weight had been lifted. Another minute passed.

"Well Christopher, can I buy you a beer?" I cautiously asked.

"I'd sooner have bourbon. I think you owe me that." A small smirk appeared as his anger and nervousness subsided even more.

"Oh, a man after my own heart, bourbon it is." I gestured to Sam who had maintained a continuous gaze in our direction for the duration of this brief conversation, since he had moved to the bar. Approaching, I couldn't help but notice his large frame. "Sam, may I introduce to you Christopher, my son. Seems he and I have a lot in common. For starters, bourbon, let's get a bottle over here." Sam enclosed his huge hand around Christopher's.

"It's real nice to meet you, Christopher," said Sam glancing in my direction and shrugging his shoulders as if to say 'well what the hell'. Turning back towards the bar he said, "I'll get a bottle and three glasses."

"You and me have a lot to talk about I reckon. Might be he'll be back on his feet in a minute getting another bottle." Still not completely at ease, Christopher smiled at my quip.

"So, has life been kind to you? Your mum, is she, she still

got that wicked sense of humour?"

"She's good. She said to say hello, and did you get what you were looking for?"

One of the last things I said to her as I slammed the door, was I was going off to find a better life than what was there on offer in England. "Mind you, I don't know if she was joking or not. As you say, she has got a wicked sense of humour." I nodded.

"I take your point. Where you staying and how long have you been here?"

Sam put the three glasses on the table and filled each to more or less the brim. I watched as Christopher gripped his between thumb and third finger and threw it down his neck in one. I nodded in an approving manner.

"Now I know he's your son, Joe. Wonder where he got that from?" Sam blurted out with a laugh in his voice. Necking mine, we all of us laughed. The tension had gone. Bourbon sometimes does that. At least that's what I tell myself.

"Have you eaten yet, Christopher?" I asked. "It's just I know a really good seafood place down on the quay. Not just good food but some really good company. There's always a surprise in store. I think you'll like it and I also think you'll have a lot in common with the owner."

Sam shook his head smiling as he did. "You really think that's a good idea, Joe? I mean, the Pantry, after a long busy day. That owner can get real fiery."

I thought momentarily.

"Oh she'll be fine. Look, she is used to my little surprises. Just think how she dealt with the last one I sprung on her." Looking towards Christopher I asked again, "Well you hungry?"

"I am as it happens. I got a snack around mid-afternoon when I got here. I've been looking for you since then. But I don't want to start any trouble. It was hard enough confronting you. I don't think I could deal with any more confrontation today. Especially as I don't know what exactly was the last surprise you sprang on this woman." Smiling broadly I assured him all would be fine.

"Just prepare for a long night and a lot of emotion! Tonight will hopefully be the start of many to come. Drink up, let's go."

THE END

About the Author

Anthony Moss is married with family and has lived in Dorset all his life.

Having left school he went into the motor industry, going on to work as a 'Technical Training & Sales Representative' for an international vehicle paint manufacturer. Various sales roles followed in differing industries and currently he works for the Apprenticeship Team at Bournemouth and Poole College

This is his first novel, based on his own interest and fascination of travel, architecture, art and Second World War history. This story combines all aspects of these topics.